# Satin in the Snow

# Satin in the Snow

Jeanette Gilge

**WinePress Publishing**
MUKILTEO, WA 98275

Satin in the Snow
Copyright © 1997 by Jeanette Gilge-Barnes

Published by WinePress Publishing
PO Box 1406
Mukilteo, WA 98275

Cover by **DENHAM**DESIGN, Everett, WA

All rights reserved. No part of this publication may be reproduced, stored in a retrieval system or transmitted in any way by any means, electronic, mechanical, photocopy, recording or otherwise, without the prior permission of the publisher, except as provided by USA copyright law.

Printed in the United States of America.

Library of Congress Catalog Card Number: 97-60465
ISBN 1-57921-016-3

*With grateful memories of*
*my grandmother*
*Emma Meier*
*"Emma" in this book*

# 1

The May morning sunshine had already gilded the box elder tree when Jeanie stretched and looked out her window. She was about to turn over and sink back into sleep when she remembered, *This is my last morning home!*

A shiver of apprehension skittered down Jeanie's arms. She had never been on a train before and wondered what it would be like on the swift Hiawatha. At least she wouldn't be alone.

Kenny's mother was going to Chicago, too, to see her other son, Ray—two years older than Kenny—before he went into the army. The very word "army" made Jeanie wince, but surely Germany and Japan would soon be soundly defeated and Kenny would never have to go into service.

Jeanie's thoughts picked up where sleep had cut them off last night and she hugged her pillow with a delighted little cry. Tonight she would be with Kenny! Of course they wouldn't be able to see each other every day because she would only have Sundays off from her housekeeping job in Skokie, but Kenny said he would phone her every noon from work. After not hearing his voice for weeks on end last winter while she finished high school and he worked in Chicago, talking to him every day would be wonderful and being with him would be heavenly.

She glanced at the small ivory alarm clock. Only a little after eight. Two more hours before Kenny's mother and aunt came to pick her up in time to catch the train at Tomahawk.

Her bags were packed, her clothes laid out. Two hours would seem like weeks. If only Gram could hear better. There were still many things she wanted to say to her. The recent scene when she had screamed at Gram was still all too vivid. The tension had built every time Gram scolded her until she could choke back her resentment no longer.

*Maybe it was good I did explode,* Jeanie thought. *If I hadn't, I would not have heard her say she really does love me and she would not have known how much it hurt me that she never praised me.* Gram had explained that they were always careful not to praise the children for fear they would be over-confident—or, as she expressed it, "Get the big-head." That reasoning still didn't make sense to Jeanie, but it helped explain why Gram never made a fuss over any of her achievements.

※

Emma shoved sticks of wood into the stove and stirred the oatmeal. She glance up at the vent in the ceiling. In a few minutes, she would call Jeanie.

Back and forth between the little cupboard and the table she shuffled, setting out the sugar bowl with the

# Chapter One

pink roses, the glass spoon holder, bowls and silverware. This noon, she would sit alone at this table.

It was eighteen years since she had taken Jeanie home—a week before Emmie died—and all those years she had asked God to let her live until Jeanie was through school. Now, Jeanie not only had graduated from high school, but was leaving for Chicago.

Sunday, at church, Mrs. Andrea had shouted in her ear, "Oh, Emma, I know how much you'll miss her, but it's time you take it easy now. We aren't spring chickens anymore!"

Emma smiled, remembering how she had nodded and said, "You're right. I'm seventy-three. That's really an old hen!"

Her smile faded when she thought of the future. For the first time in over fifty years she would have no one to cook and care for. Of course Roy and Helen and their four children were in the other part of the house, but they were not her responsibility.

She had tried to hide her disappointment that Jeanie was leaving for Chicago so soon after graduation. She had hoped they could visit some of the families together, take a walk down by the river and over to where the old house once stood—things like that. But when the job opportunity came, Jeanie couldn't refuse it.

Emma chuckled to herself. She knew very well Jeanie wasn't nearly as excited about starting that job as she was about being near Kenny again. Jeanie had never said anything about their getting married but, had Emma been a betting woman, she would have bet her bottom dollar they would be married within the year. Yes, they were young, but as far as she could see, it would be good for Jeanie to have her own home in case Kenny had to go in service. There was no doubt in Emma's mind that those two were made for each other. It had broken her heart to watch Jeanie's sad face all winter. The fact that they had no money didn't bother Emma either. "We all started with nothing," she had often told her children when they fretted because they had so little money to establish a home. "I hardly know anyone who had anything but the willingness to work when they got married. Working together and waiting for things isn't going to hurt a marriage."

---

Jeanie stretched again and yawned. Two long hours. She wished she could get dressed and leave right now.

She reached over to the night stand where her diploma stood in its black suede folder. She opened it and stared at the picture of Rib Lake high school and thought of how large the two-story building had seemed that first day of school four years ago. It had taken six weeks for Kenny to discover her. From then on, he was there when her bus came in the morning and waiting until she was back on it at night—unless he was involved in basketball or wrestling. But, he had graduated last spring and gone to work in Chicago, leaving Jeanie desolate.

Now, she too, had graduated. She smiled with satisfaction as she read, "This certifies that...," and there was her name impressively printed, "has satisfactorily completed the course of study prescribed by the board of education for the high school and is therefore entitled to this diploma. Given at Rib Lake Wisconsin this 14th day of May, 1942."

It was time to put it away. It was time to think of the future, not the past.

Jeanie got out of bed and lifted the lid of the cedar chest that had belonged to her mother. What better place

## Chapter One

for it? She laid it on the box of her baby clothes Gram had kept for her, patted a stack of pillowcases she had embroidered, and smoothed a stack of flour sack dish towels, also embroidered. She was tempted to take all her linens out and admire them, but they were so neatly stored she decided not to disturb them. How soon, she wondered, would she actually be using them.

She was about to close the lid when she saw the little box that had once held chocolates, but now held precious letters written by her father and mother. She opened it and found her favorite letter; the one written a few days after she was born. Even though she had almost memorized it, she scanned the pages until she came to the part where her mother described her:

*She only ate once last night and now she has been sleeping for about five hours, but she's trying hard now to wake up. She is so cute when she sucks her thumb. Her hair is dark brown, her eyes dark blue. Her nose is like mine and her chin is little and pointed but hasn't got a dimple like our family. Her eyes and mouth are like Ed's. Oh, yes, she's a wonderful child! Better than all the rest. Ha!*

*I was kind of sick yesterday and had a temperature. Doctor said this morning that I should never give him such worry again. He came out first thing this morning and was relieved to see how I had changed so there is nothing to worry about now.*

Tears blurred the handwriting as Jeanie tucked the letter back in its envelope. She knew the story so well. A day later, her mother's temperature had soared and her stretcher had been loaded into the baggage car of the Soo Line train for the sixty-mile trip to Ashland Hospital. For five weeks she struggled to live, but there were no drugs to fight the infection; and, May tenth, nineteen-year-old Emmie's life slipped away.

Jeanie remembered Gram telling her, "A week before she died she told your father, 'If Mama comes she can take the baby home with her, but I won't let her go with anyone else.'"

Gram had never been able to repeat Emmie's words to her that day without her voice breaking. "She told me, 'You took good care of us and I know you will take good care of her, too.'"

"Jeanie! Time to get up!" Gram called. Jeanie started and hastily put the letters back in the box. She reached for a tissue and blew her nose. There was no more time to think of the past this morning.

Jeanie snatched the big china water pitcher from the wash stand and, as she ran downstairs, she thought of the luxurious baths she had enjoyed at Kenny's sister Vi's house when she had visited last October. She wondered if she would have a bathroom of her own at her new housekeeping job.

Emma did not hear Jeanie come down, but when she turned from the table, she saw her by the mirror taking out her aluminum hair rollers.

Emma shook her head. "Never could understand how you can sleep on those things!"

Jeanie rolled her eyes and Emma sighed. "I know! I *always* say that!" Only last week, Jeanie had confessed how much it irritated her when she said the same thing over and over. The last few days Emma had really tried not to do that, but now she had done it again.

She dished up the oatmeal, stealing glances at Jeanie;

## Chapter One

hoping to store away precious pictures in her mind. Yes...she'd be able to see her brushing her auburn shoulder-length hair, turning it under in a "page boy," sweeping up the sides and pinning them in rolls. She would certainly see her sudsing her face, and rinsing and rinsing. Emma had to admit Jeanie had nice clear skin. But then, Emmie had had clear skin, too, without all that fuss.

Many people said Jeanie looked just like Emmie, but Emma didn't agree. Yes, her high cheekbones were like her mother's, but her short upper lip and smooth chin were like her father's. Emmie had a dimple in her chin like her nine brothers and she had a straight nose. Jeanie's had a slight bump from a fall on a coaster sled.

"Come and eat before the oatmeal gets cold," Emma told her. "There's nice thick cream."

Jeanie slid into her chair and Emma sat down in hers. They bowed their heads in silent prayer.

As Jeanie began to eat, Emma asked, "You all packed?"

Jeanie nodded.

"You wearing your blue suit?"

Again Jeanie nodded.

"Looks like a nice day for traveling."

Emma continued to ask more questions that Jeanie could answer with either a nod or a shake of her head until Roy appeared at the door.

He grinned at Jeanie. "You all set?"

Jeanie nodded. Not knowing what to say to him, she went to the washstand and put toothpaste on her brush.

He leaned his shoulder against the door frame. "Remember, you've got a little over two hun'erd dollars in the bank in case you ever need it."

Jeanie looked over at her uncle standing with his hands in his bib-overall pockets and said, "I hope I don't have to draw it out until...." She stopped abruptly. She wanted to say, "Until I get married," but she didn't dare talk about wedding plans so soon after graduation.

"You probably won't if your job goes good." His blue eyes beamed affection.

She smiled and nodded, wishing she could run over and hug him and say, "I'll miss you!"

But they were not a hugging family.

"Well...your room will always be here waiting for you whenever you can come home. Just write and let us know when you're coming and we'll meet you at Tomyhawk."

Jeanie wanted to thank him for putting up with her for eighteen years, but she didn't trust her voice.

Roy shuffled his feet, cleared his throat and said, "Well! I gotta get to work." He wheeled around and was gone.

Jeanie was still dressing when three-year-old Arne pounded on her door and yelled, "I helpa' you make you bed!"

"Wait just a minute," she called back as she finished buttoning her blouse.

The little boy almost fell into the room when she opened the door. "You can help me take off the sheets so Gram can wash them."

They pulled and tugged and he laughed when she threw the sheets over him. But when he poked his face out and saw her suitcase, he stopped laughing and hung his head.

Jeanie picked him up and sat down on the cedar chest. "I'm going to miss you," she said resting her cheek on top of his warm hair.

He looked up at her, nodding, "You come back!" It was not a question, but a command.

She squeezed him hard before setting him down. "I'll come back," she assured him.

*Chapter One*

She looked up and saw little six-year-old Marie watching them from the doorway with serious brown eyes. "Gram is going to be lonesome," Jeanie said. "When I'm gone, let her talk to you a lot, okay?"

"Uh-huh," Marie said and Jeanie gave her a quick hug.

"Well, I guess I'm all ready." Her eyes swept the peach colored walls, the ivory vanity dresser with the winged mirrors, the bed with the curved foot-end. "I'm going to miss my room," she said more to herself than to the two sober children. "Listen, you two run along. I thought of something else I have to do."

Reluctantly, they left.

Just the thought of her grandmother being alone made her throat ache. It would help if Gram found a note.

Standing at the dresser, Jeanie wrote:

*Dear Mama,*

*I hate leaving you but I have to find a life of my own. I'll think of you and all the things you taught me and I'll try hard to be the kind of woman you want me to be. I suppose that's the best way I can thank you for all you've done for me. Please don't worry about me. I'll write often.*

*Love,*
*Jeanie.*

She folded the note into a square small enough to fit under the sugar bowl and put it in her pocket.

Downstairs, Jeanie took fresh sheets and pillowcases out of Gram's bottom dresser drawer to make up her bed.

Gram looked up from her knitting. "Oh, don't bother. I'll wash the sheets and put them right back from the line." She motioned toward the water pail. "I don't mind if you get a pail of water, though!"

When Jeanie came through Helen's kitchen on the way to the pump, her aunt stopped clearing the breakfast dishes from the big round table. "Well, today's the day! I sure hope you like the city better than I did."

Jeanie knew Helen had worked in Wilmette, north of Chicago, before she got married.

"There's nothing more dismal than downtown Chicago in the rain," Helen said.

"There's always *something* good about a place!" Jeanie countered. She stood looking at Helen a moment, trying to see her aunt the way she wanted to remember her: crisp, wavy dark hair, nice straight nose, and brown eyes that held warmth mainly for Roy and the children.

"I know you are going because Kenny is there," Helen said, "but you better be sure that's really where you want to live before..."

"I gotta get water for Gram," Jeanie interrupted and fled out to the pump before her aunt started in on why she should date other boys.

Even pumping water was special this morning. Jeanie drank in the view of the rocky pasture and the huge, umbrella-shaped elm trees down by the river.

Nine-year-old Marilyn ran past, a baseball cap jammed down so far on her head that her blonde hair stuck straight out on the sides. "Boy, I sure wouldn't wanna be a *city-gink*!" she announced and trotted off with the shaggy collie, Buckley, at her heels.

The pail full, Jeanie stopped pumping and leaned against the smooth old pump handle. What would it be like not being able to look off at distant trees, to walk along the river and listen to its peaceful sound?

She took a deep breath, resolving to find the good in

## Chapter One

the city, and was about to pick up the water pail when she saw twelve-year-old Ronnie coming with an armful of firewood. She waited for him.

He grinned as he went past her to dump his load of wood in the box by his mother's stove.

*He'll be a pretty good-looking kid when he grows into his ears,* Jeanie thought.

When Ronnie came back out, she asked him, "Remember when you used to sit on the back ledge of the wood box with your feet on the front and 'drive' the kitchen chairs you had turned over and harnessed?"

He nodded and grinned.

"And when we had whooping cough and we pretended the cot was a sleigh?" Jeanie laughed. "We'd cough so hard we'd run to the slop pail to throw up...and come right back to play again!"

Ronnie studied the worn out toes of his black and white tennis shoes. Jeanie knew he had things he wanted to say, just like she did, but didn't know how to get them out.

"I better get going," she said. For a brief moment, their eyes met and words weren't necessary. They would be there for each other whenever they were needed.

Olga, her uncle Carl's wife, called to wish her well, but the lump in Jeanie's throat was so big she could hardly talk. Olga had been her teacher, counselor, confidante—friend. She had filled spaces in Jeanie's life that Gram, because of her deafness and her age, had been unable to fill.

"Be sure to write to Gram often," Olga said. "She'll probably pass your letters around so we'll all know what's going on. She is certainly going to miss you."

Jeanie promised she would write at least once a week and hung up the receiver on the walnut telephone that hung on the wall next to the bay window. She saw Gram outside, picking up sticks as she was in the habit of doing.

Quickly, before Gram came back in, Jeanie ran and slipped her farewell note under the sugar bowl, feeling a trifle less guilty about leaving her.

# 2

When Kenny's mother and her sister came, Jeanie hugged Gram tight and dashed for the car.

At the top of the hill, she looked out the rear window and saw Helen and little Arne waving from the pump; the girls running down the driveway, still waving; and Gram walking toward the woodshed.

In the back seat, Jeanie cried silently, glad that the two ladies did not include her in their conversation right now.

They drove along the gravel road that curved with the river and then straight north on the county-line road to highway 86. Jeanie never traveled these miles without thinking about Gram telling her how Grandpa used to make the twenty-mile trip to Tomahawk with the horse and buggy, or sleigh, once a week to sell butter, eggs, beef, potatoes—anything they had to sell.

Roy and Carl did the same thing in the early thirties,

but they had an old truck to drive. Carl and Olga stayed with her and Gram the winter they built their little log house. Jeanie could see Olga, hands cupped around her eyes, watching for Carl and Roy through the east window, fearful the old rattletrap might have broken down or had a flat tire.

It would have been nice to share these memories with the two ladies, but Jeanie still couldn't trust her voice.

---

Emma dumped her apron-load of wood chips into the box by the kitchen stove. She looked about the room for some left-behind sign of Jeanie, but nothing remained. Still, she did not cry. She needed to go somewhere else to do that, someplace where she could think and cry and pray, away from other eyes and ears either big or small.

She knew the "someplace" where she needed to go: the site of the old house where she and Al had begun their life together.

With short, determined steps, she made her way across the hayfield to the west rather than down through the spring-damp pasture. At the big slate-gray rock she sat and rested a moment and let tears run unheeded. But it was not until she crossed the next field and reached the fence overlooking the river that she broke into sobs.

Silently, the river swirled around the bend below her. Groping in her sound-memory, she tried to hear it; but the memory of its sound eluded her. Odd. She could remember how the killdeer swooping over the pasture sounded. She could even hear the murmur of the wind through pine trees, but the river sounds....

She shook her head in frustration and, in a sudden

## Chapter Two

burst of anger, pounded her fist on the rough top of a fence post.

"It ain't fair! First, I lose Al and have to try to keep the place going. Then Emmie dies and I have to start all over again with a little one. And, if that wasn't enough, I have to lose my hearing yet!"

Tears streaming, she shook her fist at the sky. "Your Word says you love me. Humph! If you ask me, that's a fine way to love!"

Instantly, in a flash of memory, she saw herself in almost this very spot about fifty years ago, railing at the Lord because He hadn't sent someone to help her when she had fallen and hurt her back. She had four small children to care for, all by herself, because Al was in the lumber camp. She could see the cattle heading for the river, single file along the icy path; and feel the pain when she had to get down on her knees to haul buckets of water up through a hole in the ice for them to drink.

She had been sure God had abandoned her and that all Al thought about was working and saving enough to buy horses.

But, God had worked things out. He had given her the help she needed that winter, and winters to come, by sending the school teacher to board with them.

Emma dropped her head with a sigh of resignation. "Oh, Father," she whispered. "I'm sorry! Forgive me! I don't understand why these things happen and I know I must trust you, but now my life seems so empty. Jeanie's gone!"

How different things would have been had Emmie lived. She certainly wouldn't be standing here grieving at Jeanie's leaving.

She caught her breath as the truth struck her. If Emmie had lived, she, herself, never would have known

Jeanie as a daughter. She would have had to watch her grow up from a distance, the way she watched her other grandchildren. Of course, they were all dear to her, but not a part of her like Jeanie.

"Oh, Lord," she whispered, "it sure does hurt to love." She sighed. "But, I'll take the hurt anytime."

Her legs ached, her head felt light. Time to walk back.

*What was Jeanie feeling?* She wondered as she walked. *Was she crying, too?* At least she didn't have to be alone on the trip. She and Kenny's mother seemed to have such a good time together. If only she could have laughed and talked with Jeanie like that!

Back at the gray rock again, Emma sat to catch her breath. Was Jeanie wishing she could turn back?

She stared at the white frame house with the elm trees towering over it. A smile hovered on her lips. No! By now, thoughts of home were dim for Jeanie and she was bright-eyed and eager to see Kenny, that blue-eyed young man she loved so much.

Emma smiled when she remembered the two of them together. She had seen a good many couples in love in her day; all those private glances, eyes locked in mutual admiration. And now she had seen it again. Oh, how those two delighted in each other!

And now they would be together as often as they could manage until—Oh, Lord forbid—Kenny would have to go into the service.

For a few moments after they boarded the train, Jeanie was too fascinated by her surroundings to think about home. They stowed their luggage in racks above their heads and settled down in the comfortable dark green seats.

Kenny's mother beamed a smile at Jeanie. "Is this your first train ride?"

## Chapter Two

Jeanie nodded, still not sure of her voice. She wanted to tell her companion how glad she was to be with her, but she couldn't risk talking yet.

"We change trains at New Lisbon," Kenny's mother said, securing a pearl earring and patting her dark hair in place. She looked at her wrist watch. "Oh, we have a long while before that. We change about four o'clock."

"I think I'll go to the rest room," Jeanie said. She hurried down the aisle of the swaying car and then, safely behind the metal door, let out the sobs she had been choking back. *Oh, Mama! I wonder if you're crying, too.*

She could see Gram walking across the yard, see her coming back into the empty room. Choking back a new flood of tears, Jeanie dabbed her eyes with cold water and put on fresh lipstick.

As she made her way back up the aisle, she could hear the coal locomotive chugging up ahead and the whistle's lonely wail.

Her companion smiled warmly as Jeanie sat down, then reached over to examine the lapel on her jacket. "I suppose you sewed this, too!"

Jeanie nodded. "I hardly own anything ready-made, except sweaters."

"You certainly are an accomplished young lady. Your Grandma must be very proud of you."

Jeanie didn't reply. The memory of all the years Gram had never shown approval of her accomplishments still hurt. The past winter had been the worst, especially when Gram squelched compliments other people gave her. Often, Jeanie boiled with resentment; but she didn't allow herself to show it, not until the day she had gotten an A-plus on a short story she had written for an English assignment. Gram had been watering plants in her bedroom when Jeanie had burst in, flushed with excitement.

The story had been passed around and all day the other girls had told her how good it was.

She shouted the good news at Gram and added, "Everyone thinks I should be a writer!"

"Humph!" Gram had snorted. "Such nonsense! You'd do better studying world history than writing silly stories!" She reached over and pinched off a tip of the red begonia.

Jeanie's long pent-up resentment boiled over. "That's just what you do to *me*!" she exploded, pointing to the pinched plant. "You cut me down every time I get a compliment."

Once the words started to come, Jeanie had been unable to stop them. "It isn't my fault I was born or that my mother died because of it! I know I'll never be perfect like she was, but you could at least give me a chance. But, no! All you ever do is tell me what I do wrong!"

Jeanie would never forget how Gram had staggered backward to sit down hard on the edge of her bed, stunned by the sudden outburst.

"Jeanie! I never knew you felt like this!" She began to cry. "Oh, girl, if you only knew how much I care about you...how proud I am of you!"

"Well, you sure have a funny way of showing it!" Jeanie had shouted before storming up the stairs to her room.

It had taken quite a few days before they had been able to talk it over without tears.

"You were always so quick to point out my mistakes," Jeanie told her, "but I can't remember you ever telling me I did something right."

"Oh, my goodness, girl," Gram had groaned, "that's what mothers are for, to show children where they're

## Chapter Two

wrong. Don't you see? I *couldn't* praise you. That would have made you proud and pride is a terrible thing."

Gram had gone on to tell her that they had always been careful to avoid praising any of their children, or to let them know they were loved. "Once a child knows you love them, they'll try to get away with most anything," she had added.

Finally, Gram had been able to convince Jeanie that her intentions had been good and that she truly did love her.

For as long as she could remember, Jeanie had believed that what Gram did and said was always right. But this time Gram must be wrong. How could it possibly be right to make her feel like she couldn't do *anything* right? How could it possibly have been right to keep her wondering if she was loved? She loved Gram in spite of all the misunderstanding and now, as the train took her farther away by the minute, her throat ached.

She snapped back to the present when she heard the voice beside her, "Kenny told me you got straight A's in school, too."

Jeanie turned from the window and her painful memories. "Yes," she admitted, "but not in typing. I'd get so nervous the page would be full of mistakes. I hope I *never* have to type again."

"Now that's the way I feel about sewing," the older woman confided. "I can knit and crochet, but I get so nervous..." Her right hand fluttered and she fingered her three-strand pearls. "Well, we just have to do what we're good at, that's what I always say."

After two hours the once-comfortable seat became less comfortable. They had talked about every imaginable subject, it seemed. She closed her eyes and tried to doze.

But Kenny's mother still had things to say. "I'll never

forget that day, the fall of thirty-eight, when Kenny came home grinning from ear to ear. 'Found my girl today, Ma!' he said. 'She's real pretty! Lives with her grandmother and teaches Sunday school.'"

*Pretty?* Jeanie thought. *I don't feel pretty. My nose is crooked and I have such a mousy little face.*

But, Kenny had called her "my girl," and at that, a wave of sheer joy engulfed her.

She would never forget that evening Kenny had noticed her after a basketball game. When he walked with her downtown to meet her cousin who was to drive her home, they laughed and talked as freely as though they had known each other for ages. After that they had been together in school day after day, and that first attraction had grown into love. Their friends said they were "made for each other," but the fear that they might someday break up had tortured her. Now, after four years, that fear had been replaced by one even worse: the fear he would have to serve in the armed forces.

Four o'clock came and they changed trains. By then, thoughts of home were long behind Jeanie.

"Kenny and Ray will be at Union Station to meet us," said their mother. "The train doesn't get in until after seven, so they'll have time to get down there after work." She gave her head an impatient little shake. "I don't even want to think that this is Ray's last week before he goes into the army. I never thought one of my boys would have to go off to war." She tried to keep her voice steady. "Oh, I hope this thing is over before Kenny is old enough to be drafted!"

Jeanie couldn't even answer. A chill raced down her spine. *Not Kenny! He just can't go off to war!*

As the train entered the heart of the city, it slowed and

## Chapter Two

slowed until the clackerty-clack of the rails gave way to creaks and groans as they eased around curves.

Jeanie stared out the window. Rooftops. Little gray houses side by side—blocks and blocks of them. Then woods! A river!

"Look!" she exclaimed, delighted to see some green.

"Forest preserves," her companion explained. "There are acres and acres of woods and meadows along rivers and creeks throughout the suburbs."

*Oh, I hope I can live near one of those forests,* Jeanie thought. As the buildings became higher, she shuddered at some ugly, old, red-brick walls with soot-blackened windows patched here and there with plywood. She also saw a stretch of narrow two-story houses and then huge apartment buildings.

The buildings became so tall, all she could see were walls, mostly gray. She felt as if they were closing in on her. How would she ever stand all this gray and grime?

When the train eased into the dim station, Jeanie began to tremble with excitement. A few minutes and she would be in Kenny's arms!

The walk to the gate seemed endless and all Jeanie could see were the people in front of her. Then, suddenly she was blinking in the light, Kenny was grabbing her suitcase and pulling her off away from the crowd. "Hi, Baby!" He kissed her quickly before greeting his mother. Jeanie managed to give Ray a hug before they all hurried off to the escalator.

On the elevated train, Jeanie could not keep her eyes from Kenny. Still, she was sorely aware of the rickety porches and bedraggled clotheslines outside the window as the "el" sped by.

As they walked down Mozart street with its high, narrow houses and tiny squares of sparse grass, Jeanie felt as dismayed as she had last fall when she had visited with Kenny and stayed with his sister, Vi, and her husband, Art.

But once inside the brightly lit and spotless white kitchen, her spirits rose. Pretty little Vi greeted them warmly and Art boomed out his welcome. This time, Jeanie didn't cringe at his loud voice.

"Hi, honey!" Jeanie exclaimed as she picked up two-year-old Merle Ann. Her tiny dark head nodded and she gave Jeanie a shy bedimpled smile. Jeanie beamed a smile at Kenny that said, *Isn't she adorable!?*

Kenny grabbed little Buddy as he was running past. The boy hugged Kenny and peeked at Jeanie with huge blue eyes.

Jeanie smoothed his blonde hair. "Oh my goodness, you grew!"

"And look at this little guy," Kenny's mother said, holding six-month-old Billy close.

"Ohh, is he cute!" Jeanie patted his fat little cheek.

The baby stared at her with serious round eyes and then gave her a four-toothed grin.

Jeanie saw that nothing in the small apartment had changed since her visit. The same gray and maroon drapes hung at the two high living room windows, the same afghan covered the worn hide-a-bed and the same hand-woven rugs hid threadbare spots on the carpet. But, in spite of its shabbiness, the place was comfortable and attractive because every inch was incredibly neat and clean. *Will I ever be able to keep house like this?* she wondered.

During the evening, Kenny either held her hand or kept his arm around her, as if he feared she might suddenly vanish.

That night, after Kenny and Ray had gone back to the

## Chapter Two

YMCA and she was bedded down on Vi's living room hide-a-bed, Jeanie floated in a lovely haze where gray and grime were forgotten and nothing existed but herself and Kenny. They had made it through their long separation. Now, all that mattered was being together.

# 3

Emma woke with a start. *Oh my goodness! Did I oversleep? Jeanie will be late for school.*

Suddenly, she remembered yesterday and she gasped at the realization, *Jeanie was gone.*

Her first impulse was to burrow into her pillow and have a good cry. But, she knew she must look to the future and not let herself sink into a pit of self-pity.

Like any other morning, she built a fire so she could make coffee before she got dressed. It had been warm enough to let the fire go out during the night, but now she shivered in the May morning chill.

As she dressed, she remembered that Olga had invited her to come over today and Carl would pick her up around nine. Olga knew how lonely she would feel, and that she would need to think about something besides Jeanie. *Bless her, Lord, for bein' so thoughtful.*

## Chapter Three

As the Cream-of-Wheat was cooking, Emma set her solitary place at the table where Jeanie always sat so she could see out both the north and east windows. Her cereal done, she went to the cupboard for sugar. When she picked up the bowl, a piece of folded paper popped up.

*What on earth?* She couldn't remember putting anything there.

She unfolded it, saw it was a note in Jeanie's handwriting, and sat down in the rocker to read it.

Her lips moved as she read each word, once...then again. The second time she had to blink tears away. She leaned her head back and repeated one precious sentence. "I'll think of you and all the things you taught me and I'll try real hard to be the kind of woman you want me to be."

Emma knew her cereal was getting cold, but that didn't matter. Right now, she needed to thank God for letting her know that Jeanie knew why she had been so firm, and that she still loved her. She needed to thank God again for helping her with the task that had seemed so heavy eighteen years ago. Most of all, she must ask Him to let her know what He wanted her to do now that Jeanie was gone.

On Sunday, Kenny went with Jeanie on the long el-train ride up to Skokie to begin her new job as housekeeper.

"I was so excited when Mrs. Winston wrote and said I could take Pat's place. Now, I'm so scared. I wish Pat's sister had never told me about this job," Jeanie said. She clung to Kenny's arm, hoping it might stop the nervous fluttering in her stomach.

"I hope Pat can stay a few days, at least until I know what I'm doing."

"Oh, she will," Kenny assured her. "Her wedding isn't for a few weeks. How long has she worked for this lady?"

"About two years."

"Long enough to be able to tell you what to watch out for."

"What do you mean, 'watch out for'?"

"Ah...well, I mean, people have their own ways of wanting things done."

Jeanie's knees felt weak when they got off the el and walked down the long flight of stairs to the street. She tried to keep up with Kenny as they searched for the right building.

"They all look alike," Jeanie observed as they passed rows of yellow-brick, three-story apartment buildings.

Eventually they found the right building. Kenny shifted her suitcase to his other hand. "I suppose we should go to the rear."

Jeanie nodded and followed him through a tunnel-like passage between two buildings. Her heart beating furiously.

Gray painted stairs led up and up inside the building's rear. Before they reached the third landing, Jeanie's legs felt as if they might fold under her. "Wait a minute!" she panted. Kenny didn't seem a bit tired.

When they found the right door, they rang the bell and stood waiting; staring at the gray door.

They heard children's voices and running feet.

"I didn't know she had kids!" Kenny whispered.

Jeanie nodded. "A boy and a girl, but they've been with her mother since her divorce about a year ago. They must be visiting."

Jeanie arranged her face in what she hoped was a confident smile for whomever opened the door.

It flew open and a round-faced blonde girl, nearly as

tall as Jeanie, stared at her. A small chubby boy stood beside her, his mouth hanging open.

For just a moment, the girl studied her with cool, gray eyes before she said, "Are you the new girl from Wisconsin?"

Jeanie gulped and nodded.

"MOTHER!" the girl shouted. "The *girl* is here!"

Awkwardly, she thrust out her hand and said, "I'm Cindy, and this brat is Roger."

Jeanie shook the girl's hand. "I'm Jeanie and this is my boyfriend, Kenny." *I'm glad you two aren't going to be here all the time,* she added in her mind.

From where she stood, she could see into a large dining room and on to an elegantly furnished living room. Out of another room came a tall blonde woman in a tailored navy suit. Even before she reached them, Jeanie could see she had the same cool, gray eyes as her daughter.

"Hello," the woman said without any hint of warmth. "You must be Jeanie." She looked at Kenny. Her penciled eyebrows went up.

"Ahh...this is Kenny," Jeanie said. She didn't dare add *my boyfriend,* and certainly not *fiancé.* "He helped me carry my things."

Mrs. Winston looked down at the one suitcase. "You can bring it in here," she said and led the way to the rear of the big apartment.

They followed Mrs. Winston through the kitchen to a room off a small hallway. Jeanie caught her breath. White and gold matching furniture stood against soft-blue walls. The bed had a pretty blue flowered bedspread. Mrs. Winston threw open a closet that was half the size of Jeanie's bedroom at home.

"I'm sorry this apartment doesn't have a maid's bathroom. You will have to share ours, but I expect you to keep all your toiletries and your towels in your own room." She nodded toward the bare windows. "I haven't had time to get the curtains back up."

"Wh...where is Pat?" Jeanie asked, looking anxiously past her employer to the doorway.

"Oh, she said to tell you she was sorry she had to leave before you came. She left yesterday." Mrs. Winston turned to leave the room. "You two say good-bye now, and then I'll show you around."

"Could I give Kenny your phone number, please?"

The woman rattled off her number as Jeanie dug in her purse for pencil and paper. When she had to ask her to repeat it, Mrs. Winston frowned.

"You're going to do fine!" Kenny assured her, and hugged her tight. "If the kids are living here it might even help. The girl could clue you in to how her mother likes things done."

When he was gone, Jeanie blinked back tears. Then she took a deep breath and went into the kitchen where she heard the children's voices.

Mrs. Winston was seated on a kitchen stool with a notebook on the counter in front of her.

"Sit down," she told Jeanie, nodding to a chrome kitchen chair. "If you do as well as the other Wisconsin girls, I'll be happy. I've had three so far. They certainly know how to work."

The children jabbered and squabbled behind Jeanie until their mother ordered them out of the room.

"Now then," she said, pencil poised, "school is out, so Cindy will be here to answer any questions you may have. Roger still naps after lunch, but I expect you to take him down to the playground for at least an hour after he wakes up. He may ride his tricycle when you go to the grocery store. There is a Jewel Tea Store a few blocks away.

## Chapter Three

Cindy will show you where it is." She handed Jeanie the notebook. "At least for a while, I will plan each menu and write a shopping list."

Jeanie nodded as the woman spoke. "You will send the linens out to the laundry. The laundry man comes on Tuesday. Our personal laundry, as well as your own, you will do in the basement. I'll take you down there, later. Our time to use the laundry room is Wednesday forenoon. I have a washboard and soap, clothespins and so on in my storage area. Be certain that everything is put away and *locked* when you are finished."

On and on the instructions went until Jeanie's head was swimming. She longed to go to her room where she could think it all over and plan her work for the next day.

She was barely in her room when there was a knock on the door.

When she opened it, Cindy brushed past her and flopped on the bed. "This used to be *my* furniture when we lived in our own house. Now, I have to sleep in Mother's room," the girl pouted.

*Poor little girl,* Jeanie thought. *This has been a rough year for her.*

"Want to help me hang my clothes in the closet?" Jeanie ventured.

Cindy hopped up. "Oh, sure. You put 'em on hangers and I'll hang 'em up."

When Cindy had hung the last garment, the dozen or so items looked lost in the big closet. Cindy looked around. "That all you got?"

Jeanie resisted the temptation to tell Cindy she had more clothes at home. Gram always said, "Don't pretend to be anything but what you really are."

"That's all!" She smiled at Cindy and put her empty

suitcase in the closet. "Looks like I better earn some money and buy more."

Cindy tossed her long blonde hair with a flip of her wrist. "When I grow up, I'm going to have *lots* of pretty clothes."

*I bet you will!* Jeanie thought.

The girl flopped on the bed again and propped her chin in her hands, watching Jeanie put the small pile of undergarments in the dresser drawers.

*This little girl needs a friend. I must be patient with her.*

"How old are you?" Jeanie asked.

"Twelve, going on thirteen. Mother says I can wear lipstick when I'm thirteen."

Jeanie closed the last drawer and sat down on the edge of the bed. "You have a very nice profile," she told Cindy.

The cool, gray eyes suddenly sparkled with life. "I do?"

Jeanie nodded and ran her finger down her own nose. "I sure don't. Fell on a coaster sled and broke it a few years ago. It left this bump."

Cindy sat up and looked closely at Jeanie's nose. "Oh, it's not so bad!" She giggled. "Anyway, I bet Kenny doesn't mind." She gave her head a little toss. "He's cute, but I wouldn't want my boyfriend to be shorter than me."

Not knowing what to say, Jeanie traced a flower on the chintz bedspread with her fingernail.

"Ah...maybe he'll grow some more," the girl hastily added, as if fearful she might have hurt Jeanie's feelings.

Jeanie smiled. Maybe they *could* be friends.

"I went coasting when we lived with my grandmother this winter," Cindy babbled on. "She lives in a little town with lots of hills. And I got to be the May queen for our play the last day of school...."

Jeanie yawned. "Do you think your mother wants me

to do anything tonight? I have to write a letter before I go to bed and I'm exhausted."

Cindy shrugged and slid off the bed. "Better ask her."

Still in the kitchen, Mrs. Winston told her there was nothing Jeanie needed to do except set her alarm clock for seven.

Back in her room, Jeanie sat cross-legged on the bed and wrote to Gram:

*Dear Gram,*

*Oh, Mama! I wish you could see the place where I'm going to work. My room is beautiful. It has white and gold furniture and light-blue walls and darker blue carpet. I've only had a glance at the other rooms, but I've never seen such elegant furniture and so many pretty things standing around. I hope I don't break anything.*

*I had a surprise, too. I thought her children were living with their grandmother, but they are here. The girl is twelve and I think we'll get to be friends. The boy is about four and doesn't look terribly bright. I'm supposed to take him to the playground every day. That shouldn't be hard. Mrs. Winston told me everything she wants me to do. She seems real nice.*

*The apartment is way up on the third floor and I can see way out over the buildings and trees from my window.*

*I'm glad Kenny will call me every day. I've never been away from everyone I know before. He says I'll do just fine. I sure hope so. At least I know how to wash clothes on the washboard. All the linens are sent to the laundry, so I only have to wash the things we wear.*

*I hope you are getting used to having me gone. At least you won't have to watch me running around getting ready for school every morning.*

*Oh, Mama, I miss you but I'll be all right. I'll have too much to do to get lonesome.*

*I'm tired tonight so I better close. Have to get up at seven.*

*Love,*
*Jeanie*

She addressed the envelope and sealed it, hoping she could find a mailbox when they went grocery shopping the next day.

Later, in bed, Jeanie's thoughts swirled with all the instructions Mrs. Winston had given her. But, the instructions didn't bother her nearly as much as those cool, gray eyes.

# 4

Never was Jeanie more happy to hear a phone ring than that first noon on her new job.

"Cindy, stay here in the kitchen and see that Roger eats his lunch," she sternly ordered. "That's probably Kenny calling."

It was.

His cheerful, welcome voice came over the wires. "How's it going?"

"Oh...I don't know. There's so much to *do*!" She sighed. "It seems the kids are staying here, but I think you were right. I don't know what I'd do without Cindy." Her voice threatened to break. "I'm so stupid! I didn't even know how to turn on the vacuum cleaner!"

"So, now you know! How's the boy?"

Jeanie glanced over her shoulder to make sure the children were still in the kitchen. "I think he's...well...a little slow. He's four and doesn't even know how to pull on his socks, much less dress himself. It's like trying to dress a wooden doll without joints. He won't bend his arms or his legs. Cindy can't stand him. I feel really bad about that, but I have enough to do without trying to get the kids straightened out, too. I don't know how I'm ever going to get everything done today."

"Take it easy, Honey. It's just the first day."

They talked a while longer, then reluctantly said goodbye. Jeanie felt as if she had just severed a lifeline.

She breathed a sigh of relief when Roger didn't balk at taking a nap.

Cindy perched on the kitchen stool and watched Jeanie wash dishes. "Want me to sing the song I sang when I was May queen?"

"Oh...sure!" Jeanie said, glad that the song wouldn't demand an answer. She longed to run into her room and stretch out for just a minute, but she had a long list of things to do before she started dinner.

Roger slept one hour to the dot. Jeanie brought him downstairs and his sister led the way to the playground.

He ran to a swing and Jeanie helped him up. When she pushed the swing, he began to scream, so she stopped pushing and helped him off.

"He *always* hollers," Cindy told her. "But he likes to play in the sand."

Two other little boys were already playing in the sandbox. Roger picked a corner away from them where he played a few minutes before he began to throw sand at them.

"You stop that!" yelled their mother, sitting on a nearby bench. She glared at Jeanie. "Are you in charge of him?"

"Yes ma'am."

## Chapter Four

"Well, get the little brat out of there before he gets sand in their eyes!"

Jeanie went to get Roger, but he threw himself down in the sand and screamed. "Cindy!" she called. "Help me!"

Cindy sauntered over, grabbed her brother's arm and hauled him out of the sandbox. "He always does *that*, too! Let's just take a walk."

"Good idea," said Jeanie. She soon changed her mind. Roger stumbled along in front of her or in back of her, stepping on her heels. No matter where she walked, there was Roger! He refused to hold her hand and walk beside her.

Long before the hour was up, the three of them were heading back home. At the fourth landing, Jeanie sagged down on a step, too out of breath to even call to the children. When they came back down to see where she was, she got up and finished the climb.

After Roger was settled in a corner, playing with his little cars, Jeanie read the instructions for dinner. One of them was: "Cut grapefruit in sections and broil, but not until I get home."

*Broil?* She didn't have the faintest idea what it meant to broil something. She paged through a cookbook, but didn't see anything about broiling so she was obliged to ask Cindy.

When she called her, Cindy came and leaned over her shoulder. "I...I never broiled anything before. How do you broil grapefruit?"

"Oh, that's easy. You just cut the grapefruit with this little knife...." She took a small, slightly curved knife from a drawer, "then you stick them in the broiler."

"Where is the broiler?"

Cindy heaved an exasperated sigh. "You don't know

## Satin in the Snow

*anything!*" She yanked the broiler rack out from below the oven and slid out the tray. "You put them on here...right side up," she said sarcastically, "Light the oven and set it on broil. I suppose I can show you how when it's time."

With a little more of Cindy's help Jeanie managed to have everything ready when Mrs. Winston got home, including the dining room table neatly set with pale-green place mats under the yellow and green flowered plates.

Mrs. Winston's eyebrows went way up when she saw the four places. "Oh, well," she said, stripping off her white gloves, "it will be good for the children to have someone other than just me to talk with at the table."

Nearly in tears, Jeanie whispered to Cindy in the kitchen, "Why didn't you *tell* me I'm not supposed to eat with you?"

Cindy shrugged and tried to hide her smile. "I can't tell you *every* move to make. You're taking care of *me*, remember?"

Jeanie slid the tray with the grapefruit under the flame of the broiler then got up to give the mashed potatoes another stir. She sniffed! Something was burning.

She yanked out the broiler tray and saw it was the grapefruit juice that was scorching.

Cindy was right at her side. "You dummy! You cut through the rind! Take them out—quick!"

Mrs. Winston's high heels came tapping down the hall. She scowled at the smoking tray and shook her head. "Serve them right away before they get cold." She turned and led her children to the table.

"You eat like a pig, Roger!" Cindy shouted when he squished his grapefruit in his hands and then loudly sucked the juice out.

"That will do, Cindy," Mrs. Winston said sharply. She turned to Jeanie. "Remove Roger's grapefruit, please."

*Chapter Four*

Jeanie could hear his wails in the kitchen as she dished up the other food.

That night she fell into bed too exhausted to pray anything but, "God! Please help me tomorrow!"

Jeanie had thought walking with Roger was bad. The next day she discovered that walking to the grocery store while he rode his tricycle was even worse. He would ride in front of her for a while and then suddenly come to a dead stop. Next, he'd take a detour down a driveway slope and into the street. She would have to let go of the little two-wheeled shopping cart, run after him and steer him and the tricycle back onto the sidewalk.

Cindy, minding the cart, shook her head. "I'm not *ever* having kids!"

Outside the supermarket, they parked both the tricycle and the cart amid an assortment of other such vehicles lining the sidewalk.

Never had Jeanie seen a store as big as this; at least a block long, she was sure. She heaved a sigh of relief when Roger didn't object to riding in the store shopping cart once they were inside.

Totally bewildered, Jeanie looked at the grocery list Mrs. Winston had written. Back home in Ogema, Mr. Nelson or Mr. Larson just pulled things off shelves and piled them on the counter and added everything up. Here people were going up and down the aisles putting things into carts. How did they know where things were?

Cindy grabbed the list. "Here, just follow me," she said confidently. Jeanie meekly followed.

When they had checked out—another marvel that left Jeanie a bit dazed—they piled the bags of groceries into the parked cart. Jeanie ordered Roger to ride his tricycle ahead of her and then headed for home.

"Where are you going?" Cindy yelled.

"Home! Where do you think?" Jeanie snapped back.

The girl stood with her arms folded across her chest. "I can't believe you! Home is *this* way!" she nodded in the opposite direction.

"Oh," Jeanie said lamely. She turned Roger around and headed the other way.

"I have that trouble all the time. I come out of a door and I always go the wrong direction. One time...."

Cindy interrupted. "Are all people from the country as dumb as you?"

Jeanie choked back a flash of anger. "We're only stupid about the city. City people can be just as stupid about the farm, you know."

Cindy merely snorted and sauntered on.

That afternoon they went to the playground again, and Jeanie prayed for strength every step of her climb back up the stairs.

Wednesday was laundry day and Jeanie groaned at the mound of dirty clothes she had to lug down to the basement.

As she scrubbed them on the washboard, she had to stop time and again to check on Roger off in some dark corner. She decided to examine each item before she dunked it in the water. If she couldn't see any spots, she gave the garment a quick swish, wrung it out and tossed it in the rinse water.

At least she didn't have to carry and heat the water like back home. Yet, her task here in the city seemed even more primitive, because there was no rubber-rollered wringer. She had to wring everything by hand.

She was glad when the clothes reel in the back yard was filled with garments fluttering in the breeze. Surely they would be dry by the time they had their lunch and

## Chapter Four

had come back from the playground. She groaned, thinking of climbing all those stairs again.

That afternoon, Roger had the sandbox all to himself. She would have been happy to be alone on the bench without Cindy. Her ears rang with the girl's constant chatter.

When Kenny called Thursday noon and Jeanie told him how difficult things were, he said, "Why don't you quit the blasted job? Even my mother would have a tough time doing what you're expected to do, and you know how *she* can work."

That made Jeanie feel somewhat better. Kenny's mother had more energy and worked harder than anyone she knew.

"Did you ask when you can get off Saturday? I need to know when to come and get you."

"Ahh...not yet. I will ask her tonight."

Thursday Jeanie ironed all day and was bone tired even before dinner was ready.

Usually, Jeanie was on her own as soon as dinner dishes were washed, but at the dinner table Mrs. Winston said, "Jeanie, I need you to help me carry books up from the basement after you are finished washing the dishes."

When Jeanie came back down after the first load, Mrs. Winston was still in the basement sorting and unpacking. "For goodness sakes! Where *were* you?"

Jeanie's heart thumped in her ears. "I'm not used to climbing a lot of stairs," she said.

"Well, take this load up and get Roger in the bathtub," the woman snapped.

Finally done with both books and bath, Jeanie still had not asked when she could leave on Saturday. There was to be a farewell party for Kenny's brother, Ray, that night.

She waited until Roger was in bed and Mrs. Winston and Cindy were in the living room reading. Knees trembling, she walked down the hallway and stood at the door. She cleared her throat. "Ah...excuse me. I...I need to know what time Kenny can pick me up on Saturday."

When her employer looked up without her usual frown, Jeanie quickly continued. "His brother is leaving for the army and there's going to be a little party that night."

"You are free after four-o'clock, Jeanie, but the house must be clean. Oh, yes, I almost forget to tell you. You'll find organdy Priscillas for your bedroom windows in the linen closet. They have been washed, but they must be sprinkled—very damp. You *do* know how to iron and hang curtains?"

"Oh, yes," she nodded. "I'm sure they'll be pretty in there."

"I want to see them up when I get home tomorrow night,"

Jeanie stood one awkward moment until the woman said, "Well? Is there something else?"

"Ah...no. Uh...good night."

Cindy, Jeanie noted, was enjoying every moment of her discomfort. Some friend she had turned out to be!

Friday morning, before scrubbing the kitchen and bathroom floors, Jeanie sprinkled the curtains, eager to get them ironed so she could hang them and arrange them. There was a double rod she had noticed, so they must be crisscross.

When she began to iron them, she found they dried out before she could get them completely ironed. She had to sprinkle them some more and then they were so wet it took that much more ironing to get them dry. The job took even longer because she had to stop every now and

## Chapter Four

then to settle a fight between Cindy and Roger. *If only she'd leave him alone!*

Eager to get the curtains hung, she turned up the iron heat a bit. *Ah...that was better.*

Cindy came and perched on the kitchen stool to begin her usual non-stop chattering. At least she wasn't bothering Roger.

Jeanie ironed furiously until Cindy exclaimed, "Oh, Boy! Now you've done it!" She pointed to a scorched section of ruffle.

"Oh, no!" Jeanie groaned. Quickly, she turned the iron down and waited a few moments.

Cindy shook her head. "Mother's not going to be happy about that." Jeanie was sure the girl was right.

Carefully, Jeanie hung the first panel and tucked the scorched section behind other ruffles. Still, she knew she had to tell Mrs. Winston before Cindy did. She'd tell her after dinner.

"You forgot the salt," Mrs. Winston said after a forkful of Jeanie's meat loaf.

Jeanie tasted hers. "I'm so sorry!" Tears filled her eyes.

"Oh, for goodness sake, don't cry!" Mrs. Winston said impatiently. "I've forgotten the salt, too!"

Jeanie thought, *The woman is human, after all!* Maybe she would be just as kind about the scorched curtain. Before she left the table, she said, "I'd like to show you something in my room." Cindy snickered.

Mrs. Winston examined the yellowed ruffle and sighed. "Too bad you didn't wash it right away."

"Maybe it will still come out the next time it's washed," Jeanie said hopefully.

Mrs. Winston nodded before she backed up and looked at the fluffy white curtains. "They certainly do look nice." Without another word, she turned and walked out of the room.

Jeanie promptly collapsed on the bed.

Saturday afternoon, as the el clattered along, Jeanie clutched Kenny's hand. "Are you sure we're going the right direction?"

"Of course! Howard street is the end of the line. We can't go any other direction."

Jeanie shook her head. "I feel like we're going north instead of south. You know how I get that *wrong-way* feeling."

She huddled closer to him. "How will I *ever* find my way around this city alone?"

Kenny thought a moment. "Well, you'll just have to learn to trust signs and numbers, not how you feel."

At Vi's house there were so many people and so much commotion no one seemed to notice that Jeanie hardly said a word. But, when Kenny's mother said she looked tired, she admitted she had had a rough week.

Everyone, including Ray, laughed and talked as if they had all forgotten that Ray could be going off to war. All except his mother. Later that evening, Jeanie saw her come out of the bathroom, her eyes red and puffy.

"Next time you see me, I'll be in uniform," Ray reminded Jeanie when she hugged him good-bye. She had the feeling he was going to like being in uniform.

On the ride back to Skokie, Sunday evening, Kenny said, "Maybe I should enlist and get it over with."

For a moment Jeanie was too shocked to answer. "But the war will soon be over and you won't have to go!" she protested.

He didn't say anymore and she was quiet all the way to the apartment building.

"Oh, I hate these stairs!" she complained, stopping at the first landing.

Kenny leaned over and kissed her and they went on to the next landing.

## Chapter Four

It became a game—kisses at each landing. Tomorrow she would remember those kisses and maybe the stairs wouldn't seem so bad.

Monday, Mrs. Winston had a long list of tasks for her to do, including "defrost the refrigerator." Jeanie groaned. She had no idea how to defrost a refrigerator. She dreaded asking Cindy, but she knew she had to.

How Cindy loved bossing her! "First, you turn it off. Then, you take out the ice cube trays, put hot water in them and put them back. Then you take *everything* out and wash the inside and the shelves." She made all sorts of hand gestures, as if she were teaching a four-year-old.

Jeanie didn't mind. All that mattered was that she got the job done. Besides, it didn't sound so difficult.

She even hummed as she took all the food out and put it on the table. She was washing the racks in the sink when Roger came in. Before Jeanie could reach him, he had grabbed a bowl of leftover beets. The juice splattered all over the table, down its chrome legs and onto two chairs. Cindy watched her clean it up. "You shoulda' put that stuff up on the counter instead of on the table."

Jeanie gritted her teeth.

Another item on the list was: "Unpack and wash box of dishes in pantry. Line shelves and put dishes away."

Jeanie didn't even get the box open before it was time to start dinner.

At least she had dinner under control. The casserole was in the oven, carrots boiling, salad made....

"*Jeanie!*" Cindy screamed from the bedroom. "Roger's got my paints!"

Jeanie flew to the bedroom. "Oh! No!" There was a smear of green oil paint on the hardwood floor around the sheet of paper Roger had been "painting." His hands, face and clothes were also full of paint.

"Is there any turpentine?"

Cindy held up a small bottle with about an inch in it.

"Find some rags!" Jeanie ordered.

Jeanie took Roger by the shoulder, sat him in a corner and told him, *"Don't you move!"*

Cindy came back with a rag and Jeanie moistened it with turpentine. She scrubbed at the paint smears on the floor. They came off more easily than she had expected. *Thank goodness!* she sighed.

"Somepin' smells!" Roger complained.

"It's the turpentine." Jeanie told him. But suddenly, she detected a different odor—the *carrots!*

She ran to the kitchen. Too late. She ran cold water over them, but they were scorched beyond the point of saving.

With trembling hands, she went back to cleaning the paint off Roger's hands and face and changing his paint-spattered clothes.

Hurriedly, she set the table and went to get the ice cubes Mrs. Winston insisted must be in each water glass. There was nothing but water in the tray.

"What's wrong?" she asked Cindy. "They didn't freeze."

With a flourish Cindy opened the refrigerator, turned the dial to 'on' and the refrigerator began to hum. "You didn't turn it back on, stupid!"

Just then Mrs. Winston came home to an apartment reeking of burned carrots and turpentine.

She listened to Cindy describe the happenings with great relish, gave Jeanie one withering glance, and left the room.

Jeanie was writing to Gram when there was a knock on her door. It was Mrs. Winston.

She came in and sat down on the bed, her back

## Chapter Four

straight, her head high. "Jeanie, I've decided to let you go."

For a moment, her words didn't register. Jeanie had not even considered the possibility of being fired.

"I think you should find another job that requires less energy. You simply can't keep up. You can't cook, you can't keep the house clean..." She made a futile gesture.

Jeanie struggled to keep from crying.

"Now...I want those dishes unpacked, washed and put away by tomorrow night along with all your regular work, or I will not pay you. Have your things ready and, after dinner, I'll take you to your boyfriend's sister's house. Where does she live?"

Jeanie told her. "Oh, dear," she groaned. "that's way down near Armitage and California. Well...I'll drive you down there *if* everything is done properly."

When Mrs. Winston left, Jeanie sat on the bed in stunned silence. Gram had been right. She couldn't do *anything* correctly!

## 5

Constantly on the verge of tears, Jeanie somehow managed to get Tuesday morning's work done without any major disasters.

It helped to not have Cindy chattering beside her or reminding her how "stupid" she was. Cindy left Roger alone, too, and spent most of the morning playing records and reading. At lunch she was strangely silent. *What is she thinking?* Jeanie wondered.

As much as Jeanie looked forward to Kenny's noontime call, today she also dreaded it, knowing she had to tell him she had been fired.

But, when she told him, he sounded relieved. "You'll get another job," he assured her. "I'm glad you're getting out of there."

When Roger was asleep, Jeanie unpacked the pretty blue and white flowered set of dishes and began to wash them, feeling more relaxed after talking with Kenny.

## Chapter Five

All day she had tried to do each task to the best of her ability. Why, she wondered as she dried the stack of plates, did she feel compelled to do a good job? *I want my money, that's for sure. But it's not only the money. Do I want Mrs. Winston to change her mind?* She carried the stack to the freshly lined shelf. *No, I'm relieved that I don't have to stay here!*

She suddenly felt almost happy. *No more struggling with Roger. No more trying to keep the two of them from fighting. No more climbing all those flights of stairs and working so hard that I feel like I'm going to fall on my face by evening. Then, why do I feel like I have to get everything done right today?*

Before she could reach a conclusion, Roger stumbled into the kitchen still half asleep, demanding a drink of water.

*Poor, slow, little boy. What will become of him?*

At the playground, Jeanie was grateful to be able to rest her weary body while Roger played in the sandbox and Cindy sat on a swing some distance away. She was gently swaying, her eyes on the ground. Again, Jeanie wondered what she was thinking.

A shower the previous night had left the sand just damp enough for molding, and Roger was patting it into odd shapes.

Jeanie stretched her bare white legs into the sun and slipped off her sandals. Today, the time spent here was a blessed time to rest and think.

She picked up her thoughts where she had abandoned them when Roger woke up and puzzled again over why she wanted to do an excellent job today. No one but Mrs. Winston would ever know what she did today. She probably would never see her again.

"Come 'ere!" Roger called.

The peace has been too good to last. Jeanie slipped her sandals back on and went to see what he was doing.

"Why Roger!" she exclaimed. "You made a tunnel!"

He grinned up at her. "I make anodder one!"

She patted his sun-warmed head and went back to the bench.

*I have to think about what I'm going to do. Where am I going to live? Where will I get another job?* The sense of relief vanished. She folded her arms tight across her middle to ease the sick feeling in her stomach.

*What will Kenny's mother and Vi and Art say when I tell them I've been fired?* In a way, she was glad Kenny's mother was still at Vi's. Even though Vi was sweet and friendly, Jeanie didn't know her too well.

Again, Roger called for her to admire his work and she did so dutifully.

Back at the bench, Jeanie glanced at her rose-gold watch. Ten minutes more and they would have to head back if she were to have dinner ready in time. She ran her finger over the crystal of the watch and felt her stomach relax a bit. The sight of it, the touch of it was a soothing reminder of Kenny; of the bond, the commitment between them. "I don't dare give you a diamond before you graduate from high school," he had said last Christmas Eve when he clasped it on her wrist. He laughed and added, "Even if I had the money to buy one!"

They never had announced their engagement; but his parents, Gram, Art and Vi—the people who were closest to them—knew their intentions and that was enough.

*What would I do without Kenny?* A fear that overshadowed all her other fears clamped itself around her heart. *What will I do if Kenny has to go in service?*

Roger let out a wail. His tunnel, or whatever he was now building, had collapsed. It was time to go home.

## Chapter Five

Cindy came obediently when Jeanie called, but was silent all the way home, except to yell at Roger at few times when he walked in front of her.

When it was time to set the table, Jeanie set three places in the dining room and one at the kitchen table for herself.

When Cindy saw what Jeanie had done, she burst into tears. Before Jeanie could say a word, the girl ran over and threw her arms around her. "It's all my fault!" she sobbed. "I told Mother about all the stupid things you did and laughed at you! Oh, Jeanie! I don't want you to go!"

Jeanie hugged her. "It's not your fault, Cindy. Your mother could see all the things I did wrong without your having to tell her. I just can't handle all this work and you know how hard it is for me to climb all those stairs."

She brushed a lock of hair back from Cindy's forehead and looked into the tear-filled gray eyes which had regarded her so coldly a week ago. "I don't know what I would have done without your help." She laughed. "I probably would have been fired the first day."

With a determined glance at Jeanie, Cindy took Jeanie's plate back into the dining room and was almost her usual talkative self throughout dinner.

Her mother was pleasant during the meal, and even thanked Jeanie for getting the dishes unpacked and on their shelves. Still, she seemed eager to get Jeanie on her way to Kenny's sister's.

"Are you packed?" she asked.

"No. Not yet. But it won't take me long."

"Help clear the table, and then you go and pack while Cindy and I do the dishes," Mrs. Winston said.

"Thank you," Jeanie said quietly and obeyed.

As Jeanie looked around the pretty blue and white room, now devoid of her belongings, she suddenly knew why she had wanted to do her work well today. It didn't matter that no one would know. She could leave without feeling guilty. She had done her best every day, not just today. After all, that's what Gram had taught her.

The ride to Vi's seemed endless in the silent car. Even Roger was quiet. When they pulled up in front of the narrow house, Mrs. Winston stopped the car and opened the trunk while Jeanie hugged both children.

"You're a nice girl," Mrs. Winston said as Jeanie picked up her suitcase. "I'm sorry it didn't work out. Here is your money."

She laid a ten dollar bill in Jeanie's hand, added two singles, and turned abruptly back to the car.

Jeanie stumbled down the dim passageway to Vi's door.

Kenny's mother opened the door. "I got fired!" Jeanie wailed and fell into her arms.

"There, there! It's not the end of the world! Come in! Come in!"

Jeanie sagged down at the white, porcelain-topped table. "I did so many dumb things!"

Vi patted her shoulder and brought her a cup of coffee.

"My grandma always said I couldn't do anything right."

"That's not true," said Kenny's mother. "Look at how well you sew and what good grades you got in school!"

"And don't forget how you took over for your Aunt Ella while she was away last summer. I heard about that," said Vi. "I heard you did very well."

Jeanie had forgotten that. Now she thought of all the work she had done, all the potatoes she had peeled and all the bread she had baked for Uncle Henry and the boys. "Uncle Henry said you did a real good job," Aunt Ella had told her.

*Chapter Five*

"All these things are new to you," Vi added kindly. "I did some pretty dumb things, too, when I first came to the city."

Jeanie looked up at Kenny's mother. Her brown eyes fairly snapped with indignation. "I'd like to see that woman do all she wanted you to do!" She patted Jeanie's hand. "I'm glad you're out of there!"

Vi poured hot coffee for them all and said, "You're welcome to stay here until you find another job and a place to live."

Jeanie managed a small smile of thanks.

---

Emma's first impulse, when she took Jeanie's letter out of the mailbox, was to rip it open, but she waited until she could neatly cut the end of the envelope as she always did. She sat down in her rocker and shook the letter out of the envelope.

*Dear Gram,*

*It seems like about a week since this morning. I learn more every day. For instance, today I learned that I better remember to turn the refrigerator back on after I defrost it. When I went to get ice cubes for dinner there was just water in the tray.*

Emma shook her head. *Ice cubes for dinner?*

*I had a little more trouble, too. I scorched the ruffle of an organdy curtain; not too bad, though. It doesn't even show now that it's hung. Mrs. Winston didn't seem angry.*

*But that wasn't the worst! Roger got into Cindy's oil paints and got it on the wood floor and all over his clothes. While I was cleaning that up, the carrots burned. The house smelled pretty awful when Mrs. Winston got home but she...*

*What on earth?* The letter ended mid-sentence. Emma turned the paper over and there the letter continued in scrawled handwriting:

*You were right! I can't do anything the way I should! Mrs. Winston just came in and said she's letting me go! I'M FIRED! She said she'll take me down to Vi's tomorrow evening. I don't know what I'm going go do!*
  *Oh, Mama! I'm sorry! I'll write as soon as I can.*

*Love,*
*Jeanie*

*Oh, dear! Oh, my goodness sakes!* Emma pulled on her sweater. She had to walk outside. *What will she do now?*
  Out of habit, Emma picked up one twig and another as she walked and put them in her gathered apron.
  *It's my fault! I should have taught her to do things better; to be more careful!*
  Three old hens pecked at her heels. "Shoo! Shoo!" she shouted and Emma knew they were protesting loudly even though she couldn't hear them as they ran off toward the chicken coop.
  *Oh, she must have felt terrible going back to Vi's to tell them she got fired. Poor little girl!*
  A car stopped beside her. Carl's. *Oh! It'll be good to talk with him.*
  Emma waved and hurried into the house to dump her load of twigs in the chip basket by her stove. Carl would follow her.

## Chapter Five

When she straightened up, he was standing in the doorway. "Let's go sit on the porch swing," she told him. "I want you to read the letter I just got from Jeanie."

Beside her on the swing, Carl read the letter. He shook his head and shouted in her ear. "Poor kid! That's too bad!"

"It's my fault! I should have taught her more!"

"Aw...Ma!" he shouted. "How could you teach her about refrigerators!? It's not your fault!"

"I tried, but she was always flying around with her own plans..."

Carl leaned closer. "You watch! She'll do all right!"

Emma dug a handkerchief out of her apron pocket, lifted her glasses and dabbed her eyes. "Well, now I have to pray that she'll get another job and a good place to live. Poor little girl!"

Carl draped his long arm over the back of the swing and turned to face her. "Ma! Listen to me!"

It was one thing for Emma to hear a few words of reply when she had a good idea what was going to be said, but quite another when someone tried to impart a new thought. She sensed that Carl was trying to do just that and she strained to pick up his words.

"When we were young," he said slowly, "you always said that troubles make us strong...in here." He tapped his chest.

Emma nodded.

"This trouble Jeanie's having..."

He didn't have to say anymore. "Yes! yes!" she nodded. "You are right. I have to remember that. It is in the middle of troubles that we grow." She waved her hand impatiently. "Why do I always go through this same thing? I feel so sorry for the one in trouble, I forget what is going on underneath! You'd think I would have learned that lesson by now!"

Carl smiled and Emma was able to smile back at him.

He leaned close again and she concentrated on his face, his words. "Think those two will get married pretty soon?"

Emma shrugged. "I don't know, but I wouldn't be surprised. I think they want to get married before he goes in service."

"Yup! Can't blame 'em."

Emma sighed. "Think the war will be a long one?"

Carl didn't answer right away. She waited, watching the crease between his eyes deepen. "Don't know, Ma! Only God knows!"

# 6

Wednesday, Jeanie felt lightheaded when she got out of bed. She certainly didn't feel like job hunting. Besides, Kenny's mother was leaving today and Jeanie wanted to be with her until she left. She hated to see her go.

"You still look tired," she told Jeanie at breakfast. "Why don't you just rest a day or two before you start looking for a job?"

"I think that's a good idea," Vi agreed. "We can look in the papers and see what we can line up, but you rest a day or two."

Jeanie let out a sigh of relief. It would be wonderful to relax for a couple of days.

That evening, with newspapers spread on the kitchen table, she and Vi studied the help-wanted ads.

"Night work! Night work! That's all I see," Jeanie

grumbled. Both Art and Vi had advised against her taking a night job.

"There are a lot of office jobs," Vi said.

Jeanie shook her head. "I can't...I feel sick just thinking about having to type. I was so bad at typing, I never want to type again," she explained.

Vi didn't say anything. She just kept looking.

Eventually they found that a company named Stewart Warner had openings. Art said he had heard it was a good place to work, and being a streetcar conductor on Western Avenue, he could tell her exactly how to get there.

Friday morning, Jeanie's hands trembled as she buttoned her blouse. *What if I go the wrong direction? What if I get the wrong street car?*

Kenny had gone over every step with her the night before, assuring her she would have no trouble. Even so, her stomach refused to settle down as she got on the first streetcar. Heart in her throat, she stared out the window, carefully watching the street signs. Then she saw the letters on a big building—Steward Warner—and got off at the next stop.

Inside the building, she followed the signs to the personnel department. A young woman in a neat, black suit and white blouse handed her a clipboard with an application.

When Jeanie came to the part about previous employment, she wrote "none" as Art had advised her, even though she didn't feel good about doing it. But then, she reasoned, she had never had a job with a company of any kind.

She handed the application back and sat down again with about a dozen other people. Many of them were black and Jeanie tried not to stare at them. Though she

*Chapter Six*

had seen black people on streetcars and the el, they were still strange to her.

She watched people go in and out of the office for about an hour, feeling more nervous all the time. She had no way of knowing who had been hired and who hadn't. Finally, it was her turn to go in.

A kindly man who resembled her Uncle Len motioned for her to sit down. He scanned her application and then smiled at her. "Quite a change from Wisconsin, huh?"

"Yes, sir."

"Tell you what. All we have right now is night work and I don't think you should be out alone, late at night. Try to find some day work. If you don't, check with us again and we'll see what we have open at that time."

Jeanie mumbled her thanks and left.

If Art hadn't described the corner and told her exactly how to come home, she surely would have gone the wrong way.

*Now what?* she wondered on the streetcar. *All their help was for nothing.*

But at lunchtime, when she told Vi, she didn't seem at all surprised. "Sometimes people have to put in a lot of applications before they find a job. This is just your first day. What's the matter? Don't you feel like eating?"

"I have a toothache," Jeanie admitted. It had suddenly started to bother her on the streetcar.

"There's a dentist right on the corner of Mozart and Armitage," Vi said. "Do you have any money?"

"How much do you think it would cost?"

"Oh, probably about five dollars if he has to fill it."

Jeanie groaned. "That's a lot of money, but I guess I better go."

The dentist was a cheerful, chubby little man. He

drilled the bad tooth for Jeanie and chatted with her as he mixed the filling.

"You live around here?"

"Not exactly. I'm staying with friends. I just came from Wisconsin. I'm looking for a job."

"Hmm. What kind of a job do you have in mind?"

"A daytime factory job, war work if possible."

"I would have bet you'd be looking for an office job," he said, scribbling something on a business card. "Here, take this over to Mr. Morey at Heinemann's silk factory. It's just a couple blocks down Armitage. He's a friend of mine. Maybe he can give you a daytime job."

*Oh, please let him hire me,* Jeanie prayed as the dentist packed the filling into her tooth.

From his office, she went directly to Heinemann's where she showed the receptionist the card. The girl merely glanced at it and gave it back to her along with an application.

Before too long, she was called to go into the office of the personnel manager. The plate on the desk said, "Miss Duckworth." Jeanie had to stifle a giggle.

The gray-haired woman peered over her glasses at Jeanie after she had read the application, glanced at the dentist's card and handed it back to her. "You won't need to see Mr. Morey. We're hiring right now. You can start Monday morning." She wrote a few notes on the back of another card, and gave Jeanie brief directions to the floor where she was to report Monday.

Jeanie's feet barely touched the sidewalk as she walked back to Vi's. *She had a job!*

"What do you start at?" Art asked at dinner.

Jeanie gave him a puzzled look.

"Didn't you ask how much you'll be making?"

Jeanie shook her head.

## Chapter Six

"Probably around forty cents and hour," Art said.

Quickly, Jeanie calculated. Forty cents an hour for forty hours, why that would be sixteen dollars a week!

***

Monday morning, Jeanie followed a stream of workers—mostly women—through heavy iron doors and to the huge freight elevator. As it began its slow ascent, she stole glances at her fellow passengers. Most were dour-faced, middle-aged women, but there was one probably in her twenties. Their eyes met and the young woman smiled.

When many of the others got off at the second floor, the young woman stayed on with Jeanie. As she had hoped, the girl stepped off the elevator at the third floor with Jeanie.

"Hi! I'm Eva! Am I ever glad to see someone my age!"

Jeanie introduced herself to the bright-eyed, freckle-faced girl who promptly led her to the "floor lady," Rita.

Rita was a pretty, but hard-faced woman about forty. She gave Jeanie a locker key, a dark blue wrap-around apron and a small scissors. She told her to wait for Harry, the foreman.

Harry had laugh wrinkles by his eyes and curly, dark hair. He walked with a slight limp.

With his hand resting lightly on Jeanie's shoulder, he took her down the aisle between rows of black machines with huge cones of white thread on the top spikes and foot-high spools at the bottom. The place smelled of oil and hot metal. It was so noisy he had to shout for Jeanie to hear him, even though she was standing right beside him.

"This used to be a silk mill," he explained. "We've

switched over mostly to nylon now. It's used for parachutes and parachute cords. These machines give the raw nylon a twist to make it stronger." He pointed to a small blackboard at the end of a machine with numbers written on it. "This tells the mechanic how to set the machine for the right twist. Your job will be to change the spools when they're full and put on new ones at the top. Of course, things don't always go right. This is called a 'head'. When it pops up, you know something's wrong and you'll have to fix it."

*Fix it? How?* Jeanie wondered.

They stopped where a short, gray-haired, overweight woman was pushing a rack of empty spools to the end of the machine. Harry beckoned to her and she hurried over to them. She regarded Jeanie with serious brown eyes.

"Marie, this is Jeanie!"

Marie nodded and gave Jeanie a brief smile of welcome.

Harry patted the woman's shoulder and shouted, "She's our best teacher. You listen to her and I'll see you later!"

By noon, Jeanie had learned how to fix the thread when a head popped up. She also knew how to tie the special little knot, how to cut into an oil spot with the tip of the little scissors and pull off the stained thread, how to change the bottom spools, and how to replace the little wires called "travelers" that spun around the spool in an oil-filled circle.

At lunchtime, as they scrubbed the oil off their hands and lower arms, Marie told the woman next to her, "This girl learns fast! I don't mind teaching one like her."

Jeanie wished Gram could have heard that.

When she went to her locker to get her lunch, she met Eva. "Want to eat lunch with me on the fire escape?"

## Chapter Six

Jeanie was delighted.

As they ate, Jeanie learned that Eva was from Iowa and her husband worked in a war plant. He had been deferred once, but Eva was sure that if his number came up again, he would have to go in service.

Jeanie told her about Kenny and that he worked spraying paint on light fixtures. "Maybe the war will be over before your husband's number comes up again," Jeanie said.

"I doubt it. I've heard we're in for a long war."

"What will you do if he has to go? Will you stay here?"

Eva folded her lunch bag and put it in her pocket. "No, I'll go back home to Iowa," she said somberly.

That night when Jeanie went to bed, she could still see and hear the big black noisy machines. The smell of oil still clung to her hair. "You'll get used to it," Eva had told her.

The noise and machines didn't bother her nearly as much as Eva's words, "I've heard we're in for a long war."

If only Kenny had a job that could be considered critical war work. Spraying lighting fixtures hardly qualified.

He would be nineteen this fall. It was simply a race against time. Would the war end before he was twenty-one? Would the draft age be lowered before then?

Like an approaching thunderstorm, she knew the war clouds were looming ever closer for her and Kenny.

# 7

Jeanie waited to write to Gram until Wednesday evening, after she had worked three whole days. She wrote:

> *I'm actually excited about keeping hundreds of threads doing what they are supposed to. It's kind of a challenge. But the best part is that I'm helping the war effort. The nylon thread I work on is used for parachutes.*
>
> *I'm earning a little over sixteen dollars a week. I'll pay Art and Vi seven, so I'll have nine dollars left. The factory is only a few blocks away so I don't even have to spend money on car-fare. I hope to find another place to live soon, but it is fun to be here with Art and Vi. The little ones are so cute.*

That Friday, Marie gave Jeanie a note and said, "Send this to your grandmother. I want her to know how well you are doing."

## Chapter Seven

When Jeanie stuck it in her pocket, Marie said, "Go ahead! Read it!"

Jeanie read:

To Jeanie's grandmother,

I just want you to know that Jeanie is doing very well here at work. She's a smart girl. I think she's a good girl, too. You don't have to worry about her.

Marie Romanski

"Oh, thank you!" Jeanie exclaimed and gave Marie's shoulders a squeeze. "Gram will be so happy to get this! I know she's concerned about me."

The rest of that day all Jeanie could think about was being with Kenny. He was to come Saturday and they would have the whole day together.

That evening she helped Vi with dinner and talked a steady stream. She dumped a pound of white margarine into a bowl and worked yellow coloring into it with a fork.

"What I like best about this job is that I can think my own thoughts all day. I really don't have to think about what I'm doing. Yesterday, I had the best time thinking of how I would furnish a three-room apartment. I just *love* red mahogany furniture. I'd have a Duncan Phyfe coffee table—you know, with the curved legs and end tables to match—and a sofa with wine-satin stripes, a gray carpet, and gray and wine drapes."

Vi kept on setting the table, stopping every now and then to keep one of the children from falling or pulling something off the table.

Jeanie stopped a moment and watched her. Vi smiled and said, "I'm listening!"

"I'd have mahogany furniture in the bedroom, too. You know those dressers with the curved fronts?"

Vi nodded.

"Of course, I'd want matching bedspread and drapes. I didn't plan a dining room because we probably won't have a dining room for awhile."

Vi still hadn't spoken, but Jeanie was getting used to her quiet ways.

"There! It's done!" Jeanie said, putting a cover on the yellow margarine. "I don't see why they don't color it when they make it."

Art laughed at her from the kitchen doorway. "Some farmer you are! Don't you know the dairy farmers pushed for a law against coloring margarine so there'd be less competition?"

"Farmers wouldn't do that!" Jeanie insisted.

Art shook his head and went off laughing.

"He's right," Vi said quietly.

Jeanie groaned. "Well, I never knew that! How come everywhere I *turn* there's something I don't know about! Will I ever learn it all?"

Vi hoisted little Billy into his highchair. "No one ever learns it all, Jeanie, but I think you have a good start."

Saturday, shafts of sunlight penetrated the narrow spaces between the houses on Mozart street. "It's such a nice day, let's go to the park," Jeanie suggested when Kenny came. "I need to see some grass and trees!"

"You really like your job?" Kenny asked as they walked down the street toward Humboldt Park.

"Well, there isn't anything to be really thrilled about, but it's easy and I'm earning money—and I'm helping the war effort."

"You are?"

## Chapter Seven

"Didn't I tell you the nylon I work on is used for parachutes?"

"Hmm. That's great! Any guys bother you?"

Jeanie snorted! "What guys? There are only a couple kids—spool boys—and the big bosses. And there's Harry, my foreman. He's got to be at least fifty. And, of course there's Tony, the oiler who always whistles and called me 'Babe'." She was immediately sorry she said anything about Tony. "I don't like him," she quickly added.

Kenny frowned. "Watch out for him!"

Jeanie could hardly wait to get across North Avenue and into the park. "Oh, I *love* it!" She twirled around on the grass. "It's so *good* to see green after looking at dirty concrete and brick walls day after day."

"And black machines?"

She smiled and grabbed his hand. "Yes! And black machines." She glanced at his profile as they walked and felt that familiar thrill. "Oh, it's going to be a wonderful day! We have hours and hours to be together!"

They talked and laughed as they walked through the park to Division street. Later, when they were near the lagoon, Jeanie said, "You're awfully quiet. Anything wrong?"

He shrugged. "Could be. The word is out that us guys who don't belong to the union might get laid off."

"Oh, do you think they can *do* that?"

"Guess they can." He picked up a stone and whipped it into the lagoon. "Trouble is, it could be hard to get another job."

She watched him throw another stone with a force that amazed her. "Why would it be hard to get another job?"

"My age. There's a lot of talk that the draft will soon be lowered to eighteen and nobody wants to hire a guy who might be drafted soon."

Jeanie sank down on a nearby park bench. "But...but eighteen is too young to fight in a war," she protested.

Kenny shrugged. "It's either us young guys go or the married guys with kids."

"Maybe it will end soon," she said hopefully.

Kenny sat down beside her, gathered her into his arms and held her close. "Honey, we just have to take it a day at a time. No one knows how long this war could go on."

She pulled away. "You sound like you think it's going to last a long time, too," she said accusingly.

"Look! I don't *know!* I sure don't want it to, but we have to face reality." He jumped up. "Hey! Let's go get a hamburger."

She was about to tell him she wasn't hungry, but she knew she really was.

Kenny grabbed her hand the way he used to back in high school and she had to run as fast as she could to keep from falling on her face.

"Stop it!" she panted. "I can't run anymore!"

"Weakling!" he teased when she fell against him. "My gosh! I can feel your heart thumping away!"

He gave her a moment to catch her breath before he kissed her.

"Oh, you!" she said, beating his chest. "People will see us!"

His eyes twinkled roguishly. "So...?"

She leaned her head against his shoulder. "I love you so much!"

"I love you, too, baby," he murmured against her hair.

Monday morning Jeanie was working with Marie, as

## Chapter Seven

usual, when Harry walked up and beckoned for her to follow him. "I'm giving you your own machines."

He pointed out two machines she would be operating. "In a week or so I'll give you another one."

But working alone, Jeanie found, was more difficult than she had imagined. At one time she had so many "ends" down she began to tremble. Several times she dropped spools and felt as if she would never catch up. She was glad when lunchtime came.

It was good to sit out on the fire escape where the air was fresher and it was more quiet. Two older ladies joined Eva and Jeanie. "I hear you're looking for a place to board," one of them said.

Jeanie nodded as she swallowed a mouthful of sandwich. "I can't afford my own apartment, so I need to board someplace."

"I have a friend working on the second floor who's looking for a boarder," one of the ladies said. "She's a widow with a sixteen-year-old daughter. Why don't we go and talk to her when we're done eating?"

As they walked downstairs, Jeanie learned the widow's name was Mrs. Janovic. They found her with a circle of women near the elevator.

She was a large-boned, blonde lady with a friendly smile. She studied Jeanie a moment before she said, "I've already heard about you from Marie Romanski. I'm willing to give it a try. Seven dollars a week. That includes your meals and a lunch to take to work but I'd appreciate a hand around the house now and then. Oh, I don't mean you have to be a cleaning lady, but when my daughter and I are gone all day it's hard to keep up with the housework."

After her failure with Mrs. Winston up in Skokie, Jeanie was glad she wouldn't be expected to do all the work. "Oh, I don't mind helping!" she said eagerly.

"Well, how would it be if you came home with me for dinner tomorrow after work and see what you think? I want my daughter, Winnie, to meet you, too."

"Oh, that would be great!" Jeanie said. "Where do you live?"

"Up near Logan Square, on Whipple street."

"That's too far to walk, isn't it?"

"Oh, yes. I take the streetcar."

Walking home to Vi's after work, Jeanie quickly calculated. Sixteen cents a day for carfare would come to eighty cents a week. Add the seven dollars for room and board, and she would still have a little over eight dollars left each week. If she could save five dollars a week all through July and August, she'd have forty dollars. If Kenny could save five dollars a week, too, maybe they could put money down on furniture and get a small apartment.

---

When Emma read the note from Mrs. Romanski, she wanted to tell *everybody* the good news. Jeanie not only had a job but was doing well.

Now, all she needed was a good place to live. *Once she's settled maybe I can stop thinking about her so much.*

Countless times a day Emma would look at the clock and try to imagine what Jeanie was doing. At eight, when she knew Jeanie was starting work, she prayed that all would go well for her. At four-thirty, when Jeanie was leaving for home, she prayed again for her safety. Would that invisible cord that had bound them so closely for eighteen years ever be severed?

*I just have to change my way of living,* she told herself.

One morning she held the Bible with its tiny print close to the east window and read Proverbs 31, starting at

## Chapter Seven

verse 10. That passage had inspired her to try to be a blessing to her family way back when Jeanie was just a little tot. Oh, she knew she would never be able to do many of the things that virtuous woman did—like buy fields or sell her own woven cloth, much less plant a vineyard—but she saw all the things she *could* do.

She certainly could spin wool into yarn and knit mittens and socks. She could plant and care for a garden, pick berries, pick up twigs and chips for fuel. She prayed that she could open her mouth with wisdom as it said in verse 26 and she certainly would not "eat the bread of idleness." She would help the younger women in any way she could, the children, too. "Oh, Lord," she prayed, as she had so many times before, "make me a blessing to my family."

It was more difficult to be a blessing these days. Now that Roy had bought a milking machine, she wasn't needed in the barn anymore and the children carried more wood and water than she did.

One thing she could still do was help keep the children's clothes in good repair. She had urged Helen to give her mending jobs and, if she spied a missing button on something the children were wearing, she sewed one on right then and there—if she could get them to wait that long.

What was increasingly difficult for Emma to do was be patient. When she knew Helen and Roy were going to town, she would trot back and forth to their rooms to see if they were ready. It wasn't so much that she was eager to leave, but she didn't want them to have to wait for her.

One day, after she had checked several times, Roy turned from where he was working at the desk and shouted, "Ma! Go and *sit down!*"

Blinking back tears, she went to her room to sit in her rocker until they called her. If there was anything she *didn't* want to do, it was cause Roy any trouble. "That boy

*Satin in the Snow*

works so hard!" she would often tell the Lord—he would be "that boy" to her all her life. "Please don't let any of the machinery break down!"

She even prayed the cows home at night. She knew how exasperating it could be when they didn't come home on their own at milking time and Roy would have to go way down into the woods looking for them.

But, young Ron was growing fast. Soon, he would be able to help more and things would be easier for Roy.

---

Tuesday night Jeanie rode home with Mrs. Janovic on the streetcar. As they walked down Whipple street, she thought, *Not Bad! Not bad at all!*

Unlike Mozart street with its two-story buildings and small passageways between, Whipple street was lined with low, yellow or red brick bungalows. Not only that, each was fronted by a good-sized patch of grass and some even had flowers and trees.

They went in through the rear of the Janovic bungalow, first into a closed-in porch and then into the kitchen. It was bigger and brighter than Vi's, but not one bit cleaner.

The rest of the house—dining room, living room and three bedrooms—was cozily furnished, mostly in maple.

Mrs. Janovic had just begun to cook dinner when the front door slammed and her daughter Winnie strode in. Somehow, Jeanie had pictured a rather timid, large girl with long, blonde hair. Instead, she had short brown hair, a little turned up nose and mischievous eyes. "Hi, ya'!" she greeted Jeanie cheerily. "Come to look us over, huh?" She laughed a rippling laugh and Jeanie immediately liked her.

## Chapter Seven

Before they had finished dinner, it was settled that Jeanie would bring some of her things the next night after work and Kenny would bring the rest on Saturday.

That night, in bed, she remembered some lines from a poem she had memorized back in grade school:

God's in His heaven;
All's right with the world.

She knew all too well that all was not right in the world, but, in her *own* little world, the words were appropriate. Right now things were right. She had a job, a nice place to live and Kenny loved her.

# 8

Jeanie had only lived on Whipple street a week when Mrs. Janovic quit her job at Heinemann's and went to work at a different factory on the three-to-eleven shift. This meant that Jeanie and Winnie were alone until midnight, except when Kenny came over—which was nearly every night.

Although Winnie was two years younger, Jeanie was discovering she was definitely wiser in the ways of the world.

Emma was delighted to hear that Jeanie had a nice place to live; but when Jeanie wrote that the girls would be alone evenings, and that Jeanie and Kenny would be alone whenever Winnie was gone, it worried her.

## Chapter Eight

*Father, you know how much in love they are and how strong those emotions can be. Keep them from doing anything they'll regret.*

Maybe she had better write and warn Jeanie. She got out her tablet of paper and sharpened a pencil with her little paring knife.

How could she say it? She stared up at her daughter Emmie's picture in its oval frame. *Oh, Lord! Don't let history repeat itself.*

Emmie had always been a good, responsible girl, but they had been in love. She was excited about teaching and didn't plan to get married for a year or two. But, she and Ed had gotten married quickly, quietly. Much to her embarrassment, she had to break her teaching contract and quit teaching at Christmas time.

Emma could remember that moment as if it were yesterday. Both Emmie and Ed crying at her knees, "Oh Mama! It was just that one time!" No wonder poor Ed had taken her death so hard.

Emma shivered. *No! I will not think these things. This will not happen to Jeanie. Father, I put her into your care.*

No, she wouldn't write and warn Jeanie. There was nothing she could write that Jeanie didn't already know.

But, she did have some news to write:

*It looks like Helen will have another baby this fall. You know she has never felt comfortable talking about having a baby, but I think it will be born before Christmas. That will be nice. Little Arne will be three this fall.*

---

July in Chicago was hotter than Jeanie could have imagined. At home, there were hot, sunny, days; but nights were usually cool. Here, each day grew hotter and at night she felt as if she couldn't breathe. She got up from her damp pillow in the morning as tired as when she went to bed.

At work, the heat was almost unbearable. The machines themselves generated enough heat to make even warm days uncomfortable. Now, with no opportunity to cool down overnight, the heat was suffocating.

Many times a day the women would slip back to the washroom to splash cold water over their arms and faces, not caring how wet their blue wrap-around aprons were when they came out. Harry never scolded; just went around moping his brow with a handkerchief that had probably once been white.

By evening, after standing all day, the women's ankles puffed out over their shoes. Jeanie's did not swell as much as the older women's, but her legs ached so badly that last hour of the day seemed like a week.

"Hey, you guys want to go to Whealan Pool with us tomorrow night?" Winnie asked on Thursday.

Jeanie knew "us" meant Winnie and her boyfriend Chuck, who often came for her in a bright, red convertible.

When Jeanie hesitated Winnie said, "My treat!" Winnie knew that Jeanie was saving all she could so she and Kenny could get married. One night last week, Jeanie had told Winnie her plans. It hadn't taken long for Jeanie to be sorry she had confided in her. A few days later, Winnie had blackmailed Jeanie into doing some ironing for her by threatening to tell her mother to charge her more to live with them if she didn't do it.

Jeanie was fast learning that simply because someone smiled a friendly smile, it didn't mean they were always trustworthy.

## Chapter Eight

She knew very well that Winnie wasn't as eager to have her and Kenny go with them as she pretended. Last night Mrs. Janovic's voice had been loud enough for Jeanie to hear even though Jeanie's door was closed. "Winnie! How many times do we have to go through this! You are *not* going out with Chuck alone!"

It sounded like it should be a wonderful relief from the heat, so Jeanie agreed to ask Kenny. When Kenny called, he readily agreed to go.

"Man! This is living!" he shouted over the car radio the next evening as they rode up Milwaukee Avenue with the top down.

Jeanie wasn't nearly as thrilled. Her hair was blowing into a tangled mess.

When they stepped outside by the lighted outdoor pool in their swimsuits, Jeanie was not prepared to see sparkling, clear-blue water. She was used to swimming in the copper-colored river or lake water. Here was water so clear that she could see the bottom. Jeanie was definitely glad they had come.

The other three leaped in, but Jeanie stood a moment gazing at the glow of the underwater lights, the glistening bodies of the swimmers and the overhead lights shimmering on the water. She slipped into the shallow end, but then moved into deeper water to avoid the shouting and splashing children. As she did her own version of the sidestroke, a close kin to the "dog paddle," she watched Winnie swim the length of the pool with powerful strokes.

It took her a moment to find Kenny because he looked so different with his hair plastered down instead of his usual bouncy waves. He and Chuck were racing and she cheered for him even though he couldn't hear her. When he won, she waved and he swam toward her.

A bit out of breath, he slipped his cool arm around her waist. "Nice, huh?"

His eyelashes clung together in little points. "Uh-huh," she whispered.

Heinemann's hot, noisy factory was in another world.

In the car, feeling refreshed and wonderfully cool, Jeanie cuddled close to Kenny and hummed along with *Sleepy Lagoon* playing on the car radio.

"Oh, I love those words, '*A star from on high falls out of the sky and slowly grows dimmer.*' I can just *see* it! I wish I could do that...write words that make people see things. Wouldn't that be great?"

"Yeah," Kenny agreed, eager to kiss her again.

Suddenly, Chuck pulled up at a Prince Castle ice cream shop. She had seen them, but had never been inside one.

"Whatdya' want?" Winnie asked.

"Two chocolate One-in-a-millions," Kenny said, digging for his wallet.

Chuck waved his money aside.

Chuck and Winnie ran in, leaving the radio on with Bing Crosby crooning, *Moonlight Becomes You.*

"Just think!" Kenny said. "Some people live like this all the time!"

Monday, back in the heat at Heinemann's, Jeanie dreamed of that clear, cool, blue pool. What bliss it had been to ride along, listening to music with the one she loved. What a great summer they were going to have!

But, that night when Kenny came, she knew at first glance that something was wrong. "I know something's wrong," she said. "You may as well tell me."

"Remember, I said there was talk about the non-union guys being laid off?"

"Oh, no! They didn't!"

## Chapter Eight

"They sure did! I'm out of work."

"They can't *do* that!" Jeanie protested.

"Well, they did!" He lit a cigarette and took a long drag on it.

His smoking was a sore spot between them, but she knew better than to say anything about it right now.

"I've been thinking a lot today. I'm going to try to get in somewhere as an apprentice tool and die maker," he said firmly. "I've heard that's a good trade to be in. Takes a while to learn, though."

By the end of the week, Kenny still had not found anyone who would hire him because he was so close to draft age.

He phoned Friday evening. "I'm gonna' go up home for a few days. I ran into a guy from Rib Lake in a place where a lot of people from Wisconsin like to go. He's going up tomorrow."

She frowned, knowing the "place" he was talking about was a tavern where people from Wisconsin gathered.

He didn't wait for her to say anything. "I'll probably spend most of my time hoeing potatoes, but I haven't been home since Christmas."

She couldn't find words to express what she was feeling.

He continued. "As long as I can get a ride for just a couple bucks of gas money, I might as well go."

He wasn't asking her. He was *telling* her. What could she say?

"I hope you have a good trip," she finally said. "Your folks will be glad to see you."

"I'll miss you, baby. Be good while I'm gone!"

She hung up the phone and walked outside and down to the end of the block. Did he really want to get married as much as she did? If he did, wouldn't he stay and look for a job?

If only she had someone to talk to. She certainly didn't feel free to confide in Winnie.

She strolled back to the house. The week yawned ahead, empty and pointless.

The next noon, she did tell Eva how she felt. Eva offered what assurance she could, but all day Jeanie felt like crying.

That evening she took a walk over to the Logan Department Store. Her favorite place to browse was the dry goods department. She remembered that Mrs. Janovic had told her to feel free to use the old treadle sewing machine on the back porch anytime she wanted to.

In spite of her concern about Kenny's attitude toward getting married, she couldn't resist looking at wedding gown patterns. She hunted and hunted for one with a sweetheart neckline like a gown she had seen in a window. There weren't any.

Idly, she paged through a pattern book, and suddenly she saw the neckline she wanted on a sleeveless sun dress. The pattern was a quarter. She could afford that. She bought it and some green-striped material for fifteen cents a yard. She would have a sun dress for less than a dollar.

It felt good to sew again, and to see Winnie's amazement when Jeanie made the sun dress in just one evening.

Much to Jeanie's satisfaction, the sweetheart neckline was just what she had hoped it would be. The bodice fit perfectly. She smiled as she put the pattern away. All she would have to do for her wedding gown was combine it with a pattern with a long train.

She wore the new sun dress over to Vi's the next evening and Vi said it was very becoming.

Jeanie didn't say anything to Vi about how she felt

*Chapter Eight*

about Kenny going home instead of hunting for a job, but she had a hunch Vi knew.

She was feeling a bit more relaxed on the streetcar going home, until she saw a man reading a paper with the headline:

PLANS TO LOWER DRAFT AGE IN FALL

It had been a long while since she had felt so depressed. She crept off to bed feeling numb.

# 9

Three days after Kenny got back from Wisconsin, he came over to see Jeanie, grinning his carefree high-school-days grin. He had been hired at a tool and die shop, and the personnel manager had promised him he soon would be working as an apprentice.

Jeanie couldn't wait to write the good news to Gram.

*Dear Gram,*

*We're so happy! Kenny has been hired at a tool and die factory. Right now, he is working in the shipping department, but they have promised that he will soon be working as an apprentice tool and die maker.*

The next day Jeanie hummed as she worked, planning how she and Kenny would save money. At seventy-five

## Chapter Nine

cents an hour, he would be able to save some money each week and soon have enough to buy a new suit for their wedding.

"Just think," Jeanie chattered excitedly as they walked around Logan Square that evening, sharing a nickel box of popcorn, "if we keep saving you'll have enough to buy a suit...."

"Now, don't start making plans yet! I haven't even had my first paycheck," he warned.

"Oh, I know, but I've been thinking that it will cost us less to live when we're married than it does now. We're each paying seven dollars a week for rent and you have to eat out all the time.

When we're married we'll save a lot when you don't have to eat out and get your laundry done."

He didn't answer.

She quickly went on. "And look at the carfare you'll save not having to come and get me like you do now."

Kenny leaned against a lamppost, dug his hands in his pockets and stared over her shoulder. "I don't know. We better be sure to have some cash on hand before we make any real plans."

"You know I have some money in the bank. I plan to use some of it for our wedding reception. I don't expect Roy and Helen to pay for all of it. We won't be broke."

Abruptly, Kenny changed the subject. "Let's go to a Cubs game some Sunday when they're in town."

"Sure. I 'spose we could do that," Jeanie said with a sigh. She knew he didn't want to hear more of her plans.

That Friday, Harry went around to all the workers asking who would like to work on Saturday. Anyone who did, he explained, would be paid time and a half. Almost before he finished asking, Jeanie told him she would be there.

The next day at her machines, Jeanie added figures. At forty-two cents an hour she could hardly believe she was earning more than a penny a minute! Why, she would earn a little over five dollars today. If she could work every Saturday they could soon think about buying some furniture.

Harry had said they would be working most Saturdays now.

Sunday morning she wished she could stay in bed, but she was to meet Kenny at the church near Art and Vi's and then go to Vi's for dinner.

It was good to hear the familiar hymns played on the pipe organ, but the big old church still felt strange to Jeanie. The pastor had a monotonous voice and Jeanie's mind kept wandering. A few people nodded and smiled as they walked out, but no one spoke to them.

Art and Vi were pleased to hear about Kenny's new job. "Tool and die is a good trade to get into," Art assured Kenny.

Jeanie told them she would probably be working Saturdays, but didn't dare talk about the plans she was making.

At work on Monday, Jeanie put a little note pad by the end of one machine and from time to time jotted down figures. The day went fast.

She was reading on the back porch when Kenny came that night.

He stubbed out a cigarette in a nearby ashtray, gave her an absent-minded kiss and glumly sat down next to her on the day bed.

Jeanie groaned. "Oh, dear! Now what's wrong?"

He avoided her eyes, pulled out another cigarette and lit it before he said, "I lost my job."

"You *what*?"

## Chapter Nine

He took a deep drag on the cigarette before he said, "Now hold on. Wait till I tell you the whole thing. Well...there wasn't any work to do, so this guy Rocky and I went out on the loading dock for a smoke. While we were gone a load came in and the other guys were working like crazy when the boss came through." He shrugged. "He didn't even give us a chance to explain; just told us we were fired."

Jeanie choked back a sob.

"Anyway," Kenny continued, "Rocky said that apprentice stuff was just a lot of hot air; that every guy in the shipping department was promised an apprenticeship when they were hired, but some of them have been there more than a year and no one's got it yet."

"It was a job," Jeanie said sadly.

Tuesday was a long, hot day and there was no note pad with figures on it.

That evening Jeanie was too dejected to enjoy Kenny's kisses. He accused her of being cold just when he needed her the most. She explained that they didn't know how long it would be before they could be married and they had better slow down.

He went home early and she cried herself to sleep.

"Oh, dear," Emma muttered to herself as she read Jeanie's latest letter saying that Kenny's job at the tool and die shop had not worked out. Emma sensed there was more that Jeanie hadn't written.

Now Emma faced telling the family what Jeanie had written and couldn't bear to have anyone think Kenny was irresponsible.

She got up and put wood in the stove to heat water for

a cup of tea. *I'm like an old she-bear protecting her cub when it comes to that boy, and he isn't even my son!*

As she sat waiting for the water to heat, she thought how disappointed Kenny's parents must feel if they knew.

She was about to tell Helen Jeanie's unhappy news when she recalled how, time and again, she had waited a while before telling a bit of bad news and, in the meantime, something else happened. Many times the bad news never had to be told.

*Yes! I'll just wait a few days.*

Sipping her tea, she thought about how disappointed Kenny and Jeanie must be and how young people so often think every setback is the end of the world. She wished they didn't have to suffer these trials, that they could learn an easier way.

Her cup was empty, but still Emma sat gazing out through the screen door to the lawn and the tall pine trees by the road. She had become so engrossed in Jeanie's problems again that she couldn't remember what she had planned to do the rest of the afternoon.

With an impatient shake of her head she got up to put away the sugar bowl and wash her cup, saucer and spoon as she was in the habit of doing.

Because she still couldn't remember what she had planned to do, she picked up her knitting and sat down in the rocker.

"After all these years you ought to know better," she scolded herself. "Haven't you learned by now that thinking and thinking about a problem doesn't do one bit of good? How many times have you gone through this? You try to think of ways to solve the problem instead of putting it in God's hands. Don't you know by now that He loves them more than you can ever love them and has a plan for them?"

## Chapter Nine

*Oh, Lord. Forgive me again. You see their struggle. I trust you to work it out to their good the way you have promised you would do for all those who love you.*

She began to sing *Leaning on the Everlasting Arms*, and she could actually feel the Lord's sweet peace enfolding her.

Ah...now she knew what she had planned to do! Out on the porch steps her geranium slips waited to be planted.

# 10

The night after Kenny lost his job, Jeanie waited and waited for him to come. About eight, he phoned to tell her he wouldn't be over; that he had been job-hunting.

*Until eight o'clock at night?*

Heavy-hearted, Jeanie flopped across her bed. After a while she decided to do her laundry and a few other things she never got to do when Kenny was around.

But, Winnie came in before she could get up, and every time Jeanie tried to get up Winnie pushed her back down.

Although Jeanie was taller, she was no match for Winnie's strength. "*Winnie!*" she protested. "I want to do my laundry!"

"Not until you tell me what's going on around here." Winnie said with a last push. "You two have a fight?"

Jeanie burst into tears and buried her face in her pillow.

## Chapter Ten

She wasn't sure she trusted Winnie, and yet, it would feel good to tell her what was happening.

Winnie sat down and rubbed gentle circles on Jeanie's back. She could be so sweet at times. "Want to talk about it?" she asked softly.

Jeanie nodded and sat up. She took the tissue Winnie offered her.

"Well, first of all, Kenny lost his job..."

"So...he'll get another one," Winnie said confidently.

Jeanie shook her head. "It's not...that...easy," she said, still sniffling. "He's too close to draft age."

"They aren't taking them under twenty-one!"

"Not yet," Jeanie agreed, "but it might be lowered soon." That statement brought another flood of tears and Winnie sympathetically waited.

"The worst part," Jeanie continued, "is that *I* feel like I'm being torn apart. We're alone together so much now, and we love each other so much..."

Winnie nodded knowingly. "And he wants to go farther than you do."

"How did you know? You're two years younger than I am but you're so...."

Winnie laughed a wry laugh. "Let's say I just grew up early. But, we're talking about you. Why don't you get married? That would solve your problem!"

"You know we can't until we save more money!"

"Yeah. I forgot. How much do you think you'd need? I could lend you some." She grinned. "I have a few bucks in the old sock."

"Oh, Winnie! Would you really?" She shook her head. "No, that's not the answer. Then we'd just owe you. We have to start out on our own. What we really need is for Kenny to get a steady job. We need to put some money down on furniture. Kenny needs a new suit and I need money for material for my wedding gown."

"A white one?"

"Of course!" Jeanie lifted her chin. "That's always been my dream. Oh, I don't mean the dress so much as what is symbolizes."

Winnie's eyebrows went up. "You mean virginity?"

Jeanie nodded and felt her face flush.

Winnie threw back her head and laughed. "Good grief! You can wear a white dress and not be a virgin! I've seen some brides in white gowns who looked pretty...ah...round."

"I couldn't," Jeanie said firmly.

"Boy," Winnie said as she got up from the bed, "you sure have high ideals. Does Kenny feel the same way?"

"Well...yes, he wants us to start out right, but he keeps reminding me that he's human."

Tears welled up again. "See what I mean by feeling torn apart?"

Winnie put her arm around Jeanie's shoulders a moment, then grabbed Jeanie's hand and pulled her up. "Come on! I'll help you do your laundry."

Saturday evening, Jeanie and Winnie's mother talked over a cup of coffee. "You better think twice about marrying that young man," she warned. "You deserve someone with a good job and...."

Jeanie was too surprised, too hurt, too angry to answer her. "Excuse me," she said, getting up from the table. "I have a lot of things to do."

Jeanie was aware that never before had their been such tension between her and Kenny as on that weekend.

Monday at work, Mrs. Janovic's words of warning haunted Jeanie. *What if he can't ever earn a living? What if he starts drinking like some of his friends?*

She shook those thoughts off only to be attacked by an

## Chapter Ten

even worse one. *What if he has to go into service while we still have this tension between us?*

Then came the worst thought of all. *What if he went in service and didn't come back?* She thought of all the service flags she had seen hanging in windows with gold stars on them.

She was suddenly aware that the new girl being trained by Marie was watching her from across the aisle. The girl was about her age and Jeanie was eager to get to know her. But feeling so troubled the past few days, she hadn't made any effort to talk with her. Gram had always said a good cure for one's troubles was to think about someone else. It was time to meet this girl.

She found the opportunity at lunchtime when all the women were washing up at the long sink in the rest room. She squeezed in next to the girl and said, "Hi! I'm Jeanie!"

"Hi!" the girl smiled back. "I'm Marge." She had dark hair and was pretty enough to grace a magazine cover. She laughed and lowered her voice. "Was I glad to see you! We young ones seem to be a minority. I was hoping we could get to talk."

"You look like you should be a secretary or something," Jeanie whispered. "What're you doing here?"

Marge's laugh bubbled up again. "I was going to ask you the same thing!" She shrugged. "I'm here because it pays better than office work. What about you?"

"Office work is not for me," Jeanie said. She tossed the paper towel into the waste basket. "Would you like to eat lunch with Eva and me? She's the other young one."

"You mean little freckle-face? Sure. I'd love to."

Eva welcomed her and, as they ate, Marge told them that her husband, John, would probably be drafted soon. If he was, she would go back home to Nebraska. Eva told

*Satin in the Snow*

Marge about her husband, that he had been deferred once and that a second deferment was unlikely.

Jeanie listened. They certainly didn't sound happy about the prospect of their husbands leaving, but neither did they sound desperate. That gave her hope, like when the sun breaks through thick clouds just long enough to let you know it's still up there.

# 11

Winnie came home that first Monday evening in August, hugging an album with several records in it. "Wait till you hear these," she said in a quiet way that puzzled Jeanie.

Jeanie picked up the cover and read, "Fred Waring and the Pennsylvanians," as Winnie turned on the recorder.

Winnie stretched out on the sofa and Jeanie leaned back in the lounge chair as the choir began to sing *Were You There When They Crucified My Lord?*

Jeanie closed her eyes, clinging to every word. She had never heard that song before. Before it ended she found herself inwardly crying out to God, *I'm sorry! I'm so sorry! I've hardly thought about you because I've been so busy thinking about my problems.*

When she saw Winnie brushing tears from her cheeks, she wasn't ashamed to do the same.

"It's so beautiful," Winnie said softly. "I thought you'd like it. You know," she said wistfully, "when I was in grade school I wanted to become a nun."

"You did?" Jeanie had never thought of Winnie being especially spiritual.

Winnie chuckled. "But then I discovered boys."

Winnie sat up on the sofa, her face serious. "Do you think a woman can serve God even if she is married and has kids?"

"Oh, yes," Jeanie answered. "What is more important than being a good wife and rearing Godly children?"

"Did you ever want to do anything else? I've never heard you talk about anything but getting married."

"When I was a lot younger I used to think about being a teacher. My mother was a teacher."

"A high-school teacher?"

"Oh, no! She just went to normal school for two years after she got out of grade school and then taught in a one-room school out in the country."

Winnie looked puzzled. "Normal school? I never heard of that!"

Jeanie shrugged. "I don't know where that name came from."

"Did you ever think of going to college?"

"College? No! I hardly know anyone who went to *college!* Are you going to go to college?"

Winnie shrugged. "I might! I don't want to get married right away when I get out of high school." She gave her head a little independent toss. "Maybe I'll be an archeologist or something."

"An *archeologist?*"

"Sure, I'd like to work on a dig in the Holy Land. Maybe I'd get to know more about God."

"You get to know about God in your church, don't

## Chapter Eleven

you? I know you're Catholic. I don't know much about the Catholic religion. I've been to a Catholic wedding and there was one Catholic boy in my grade school, but we didn't talk about his church. I know you believe in Jesus, that's about all."

Winnie smiled. "Well, I don't know anything about Protestants except you must believe in Jesus, too, because I see crosses on churches."

"Yes, of course there are a lot of different Protestant religions, but true Protestants believe that Jesus is God's son, that He died for our sins, rose again and will come back again someday."

"We believe that, too. Why do you think there are so many different churches?"

Jeanie shrugged. "I don't think it was God's idea to have people split up in many churches, but you know how different people are, and how set they are on their own way of thinking." Jeanie sighed. "All I know is that I want to get closer to God, like my grandmother. She sings hymns and talks to Him like she really *knows* him!"

"She does?"

Jeanie nodded and continued. "It used to even make me mad because she was so happy all the time and she didn't have a bloomin' thing to be happy about! I mean, she hardly ever got anything new, except Christmas and birthday presents. She'd sit in her little rooms day after day with the same old, worn furniture and hardly ever go anyplace except to visit her kids, and she'd be so peaceful!" Jeanie lowered her eyes. "Except when she couldn't get me to put my clothes away, or get out to the school bus in time."

The phone rang. It was Kenny and Jeanie knew that meant he wasn't coming over. Somehow, after this talk with Winnie, she knew it wouldn't spoil her whole evening. She needed to think about other things, important things, not only of Kenny.

He said he had decided to take any kind of job he could get, rather than just looking for a tool and die apprenticeship and had found several leads for jobs to track down the next day.

All evening Winnie played the Fred Waring records: *In The Garden...The Old Rugged Cross*. Jeanie felt a new warmth and kinship with her. She went to bed feeling more relaxed than she had in days.

But, in the morning, her newfound peace was gone; replaced by heavy-lidded weariness and the need to cry.

As she walked to the streetcar, the tiny, well-kept lawns and flower beds she usually enjoyed seemed to have lost their charm. Instead of slowing her steps when she came to the English basement apartment she admired, she turned her head. Day after day, she had caught a glimpse of the cozy living room with its shining mahogany tables and comfortable looking chairs, dreaming of the day when they would have a room like that. But, today she didn't have the courage to dream.

At noon, Marge sensed her mood. "No job yet?"

"Not yet."

"You working Saturday?" Eva asked Marge.

"No. John doesn't want me to work when he's home."

"Frank's the same way," Eva said. "He says I have enough to do around the house."

Jeanie could understand why the men didn't want their wives to work Saturdays, but she wondered if she and Kenny would ever have enough money to make such a choice.

Friday, Jeanie watched the clock, waiting for Harry to come down the aisle to ask the girls about working the next day. He usually came right after lunch.

## Chapter Eleven

At two o'clock, he hadn't said a word; just limped up and down the aisles with his clipboard, doing his regular work. At three, still no word. Jeanie bit her lip. That day of overtime pay meant so much!

At three-thirty she went to the washroom where she heard one older lady tell another, "No work tomorrow." She went back to her machines fighting tears of disappointment.

She spent the last half hour of the day planning what she and Kenny could do the next day. Winnie and her mother had been invited to some cottage on a lake for the whole weekend, so she and Kenny would be alone. She *must* find something for them to do out of the house that didn't cost much money.

Of course, she knew Kenny would love to go and see the Cubs play baseball, but they couldn't afford to do that.

When they talked about what they would do Saturday and Sunday on the phone that evening, he said, "I *don't* want to walk around Humboldt park or Logan Square again, that's for sure. I suppose we could take the streetcar down to North Avenue Beach."

Jeanie remembered the one time they had done that. "I hate swimming in that cold water," she told him. "Can't we do something else that doesn't cost much money?"

Kenny sighed. "How about taking the el downtown and just walking around in stores and looking at windows?"

"I guess so. I suppose I could pack a lunch and we could eat somewhere down by the lake," she said halfheartedly.

"Oh, for Pete's sake, we can afford to buy a hamburger!" he said.

She hung up the phone and stood by the screen door as if there was a wall everywhere she turned. The man next door was cutting his tiny yard, back and forth...back and forth. Suddenly, the sound of the lawn mower and the scent of freshly cut grass brought back such strong memories of home that she ran sobbing to her room and threw herself across the bed.

*I hate this dirty, crowded city! I want to listen to the river and walk through the woods! I hate those smelly black machines. I hate not having money to go to movies or to the ball game, or even to buy an ice cream cone. I'm disappointed in Kenny because he lost that job and that he doesn't seem nearly as eager to get married as I am.*

*Oh, Mama! I miss you!*

She cried herself out, took a bath and went to bed; not caring if she ever got up again.

In the morning, the sun was shining and Jeanie was again glad to be alive. She even enjoyed having the house to herself and sang along with the radio as she swept the kitchen floor.

She couldn't wait to see Kenny. He would be wearing a fresh cotton dress shirt with the neck open and sleeves rolled up. He'd smell like Mennen aftershave and she'd want to kiss him and kiss him.

She groaned. One of these days she would be able to revel in that fresh shave without all those warning signals clanging in her mind!

The sun was no longer shining when she opened the door for him, and there were rain splotches on his blue shirt.

"Oh, I didn't know it was going to rain!" she said.

A sharp crack of thunder shook the house.

"Maybe it's just a shower," Kenny said hopefully before he tenderly kissed her.

"Hmm...you smell so good," she murmured and kissed him back. Then quickly, she slipped out of his embrace.

## Chapter Eleven

Kenny's predicted shower turned into a steady rain.

They read the Chicago Tribune and started a crossword puzzle, but lost interest before they finished.

They took a long time eating the sandwiches Jeanie made. Afterwards, Kenny stretched out on the day bed to listen to the baseball game on the radio.

"I'm going to do some ironing," she told him but she wasn't sure he even heard her.

About five, she made grilled cheese sandwiches and opened a can of tomato soup. They ate on the back porch, listening to the rain pelting on the roof.

Kenny helped her with the dishes, and then they stood at the front door watching the rain drip from the iron railing and the maple tree. Kenny's arms crept around her.

She leaned her head back against his chest longing to turn into his arms. Back came that feeling of wanting to cry.

She tore herself away. "Let's make some popcorn!"

Kenny lit a cigarette and puffed away, still looking out at the rain.

As she popped corn in the kitchen, she thought about ways to talk to him about smoking. How *could* he keep smoking and wasting all that money? Besides, she hated the smell and it couldn't be good for him.

When he came into the kitchen, without a cigarette, she said nothing at all about his smoking.

When they were settled on the back porch with bowls of buttery popcorn, she said, "How much do you think a new suit would cost?"

Kenny shrugged. "About thirty-five or forty dollars."

"If you pay for it in ninety days, is that considered cash?"

"Depends. Some places say thirty days." He finished a

handful of popcorn before he said, "Look! I don't have any money for a down payment on a suit, if that's what you're thinking. Don't even *think* about getting married until I have a steady job," he said sharply.

Jeanie hung her head. "I know...."

"Wanna run off by ourselves and get married when I get a job?"

Jeanie's head snapped up. "No! I can't imagine starting off like that! We need God's blessing! And besides, how would your folks and my grandmother feel? And you know what other people would think!"

Kenny snickered. "I know what they'd think!"

She rolled her eyes.

Kenny chuckled. "Ah...I was just teasing, honey. I wouldn't want to start out like that either."

The evening dragged on.

"Boy, this summer sure hasn't turned out the way I thought it would," Kenny said. "Just think, some kids are riding around in convertibles and eating at nice places...."

Jeanie snorted. "I hated that dumb convertible. It messed up my hair."

Kenny shook his head. "Women! Hey! I don't hear the rain anymore!"

The rain had slowed to a drizzle. Jeanie found an umbrella and, hand in hand, they walked a few blocks down Whipple street. She longed to walk past the English basement apartment and show it to Kenny, but decided that would have to wait until he had a job.

Back in the house, Kenny yawned. "Guess I'll go home. I'm tired." He grinned. "This hard work is killing me!"

He drew her to him for a good-bye kiss...another and another.

"Kenny! Stop it!"

## Chapter Eleven

"Aw, honey, I haven't kissed you all day!"

"You *know* I want to, but we just can't!" She tore herself away and ran to the bathroom.

Through her sobs she could hear him calling, "Jeanie, come on out! I'll behave!"

"You...gotta...go home," she sobbed.

"I'll go home and *stay* home!" he threatened.

She came out.

He was in the living room lighting a cigarette. His hand was shaking.

"Look, just settle down. I'll get a job soon. I've got some good leads for Monday. As soon as I get a job that looks like it's going to last, we'll get married. Okay?"

She longed to run over and hug him, but she stayed across the room in the lounge chair. Voice still shaky, she said, "I don't care if we have just *one room!* Just so we're together."

He stubbed out his cigarette, got up and pulled her to her feet. "Do I get a goodnight kiss or are you going to run off to the bathroom again?"

"It's not funny!" she said against his chest.

"Some day we'll think it was."

"Sure, in about fifty years," she said bitterly.

He kissed her lightly and left.

*Maybe cultures that don't allow the couple to be left alone until after the wedding have the right idea!* Jeanie thought as she got ready for bed.

---

Sunday, they went to church and then to Vi's for dinner. They stayed until evening and then each went home their separate ways.

On the streetcar, Jeanie's throat ached for a good cry.

Kenny had hardly looked at her all day and that lovely "us" feeling had been totally missing.

Monday was a long, hot, dreary day and Jeanie's heels felt as if she were walking on bare bone on her way to the streetcar.

As usual, she glanced at the headlines at the newsstand. She read:

### MARINES LAND ON GUADALCANAL

She didn't have any idea where Guadalcanal was.

Two well-dressed businessmen, also waiting for the streetcar, were talking about the war. One with a double chin picked up a paper and tapped it with his finger. "Good move! If we don't wipe out that air base, the Japs'll be crawling all over Australia," he said to the thin man.

*Why are we concerned about Australia?* Jeanie wondered.

When the streetcar came she took a seat behind the two men so she could eavesdrop on their conversation.

At first, they talked about gas rationing and how they hated having to ride the streetcar. Then, they talked more about the actual war.

The thin man thought the battle of Midway Island had definitely been a turning point in the Pacific war.

Double chin wasn't so sure, but he said the battle of the Coral Sea had certainly foiled the attempt of the Japanese to invade Australia.

Thin man agreed with that and said Australia had to be protected at all costs.

Double chin heaved a sigh. "I'll feel a lot better when there's a turn-around in Europe. Those poor devils in England! Those stinkin' Nazi's are bombing the hell out of them."

## Chapter Eleven

Thin man nodded. "The sooner we get a strong air force over there the better. England can't hold on alone much longer."

Double chin said, "Yeah! It's gong to be a long hard struggle. I don't see the end for three...maybe four years."

Jeanie stumbled off the streetcar blinded by tears. *Four years!* The world had never seemed so dark.

At home, she tried to act interested as Winnie chattered about a new guy she had met at the lake, but all the while she was thinking about what she had heard on the streetcar.

The next evening she watched for Kenny at the door. She soon saw him jauntily walking across the street with a big grin and knew he had good news.

She ran to meet him. "You got a job!"

He frowned. "Whatdya' mean? I haven't said a word!"

She grabbed his arm. "Don't tease me! I saw you grinning!"

He slipped his arm around her waist. "How's eighty-five cents an hour sound?"

"Oh, Kenny! Where? *Tell me!*"

He did not tell her until they were on the back porch. "Ever hear of Dryden Rubber Company?"

She shook her head.

"They've got a big war contract and it doesn't seem to matter if guys can only work until they're drafted. I start tomorrow—nine hours a day and most Saturdays!"

"Overtime after forty hours?"

Kenny grinned. "Yep!"

Jeanie whirled around the porch. "I'll get a calendar!"

Kenny frowned "Hey! Hold on! Let me work a few days before you start making plans!"

She pretended to pout.

Kenny grabbed her hand. "C'mon! Let's celebrate with an ice cream cone!"

Even in the dim glow of the street lights, the world looked amazingly bright and green that evening.

Jeanie took a lick of Kenny's chocolate, and he took a big bite of her butter pecan. She said that was worth two licks of his and he held it away from her.

Oh, it was wonderful to laugh again!

# 12

*Kenny has a job!* was the first thought that came into Jeanie's mind Tuesday morning. With energy she hadn't felt for days, she sprang out of bed and got ready for work.

This morning she was more eager than ever to take a peek in the English basement apartment. Now she could really begin to plan their home. But, as she got closer, she could see white over the windows, a few more steps and she saw the venetian blinds were closed. She walked on feeling cheated of the bright spot in her morning.

She quickened her pace, eager to tell Marge and Eva that Kenny had a job.

Marge was delighted. Eva was, too, but she had news of her own. Her husband, Frank, had received his "greetings" from Uncle Sam and this time they didn't think he would be deferred.

Jeanie ached for her.

At her machines, out came the little notebook again; and by noon, Jeanie had pages of figures. But, no matter how she calculated, there was never enough money. In order to get a few essential pieces of furniture and household items, money for rent, the trip up home, and all the wedding expenses—even if they worked every Saturday and saved every cent they could—it would take at least until Christmas. By that time, there could be no outdoor reception on the lawn at home and Helen would have a new baby to care for. There *had* to be a way for them to get married this fall, but Jeanie hadn't found it by noon.

At lunchtime Marge exchanged glances with Jeanie, both having noticed Eva's puffy eyes. "Maybe he'll get another deferment," Marge said hopefully. "I read just last night that a lot of women are enlisting in the WACS. Surely they won't need to call as many men now."

Eva gave her a weak smile. "Thanks for trying, but I've been reading, too, about how many men they plan to call up this summer, even though there are so many women signing up." She sighed. "They're considering lowering the draft age this fall, too."

A cold chill ran up Jeanie's spine. She remembered the headlines and the conversation between the two men on the streetcar. She almost choked on the last mouthful of her sandwich.

That evening, Kenny phoned to say he was going to bed early. He wasn't used to working nine hours a day. *Just as well*, Jeanie thought. *We shouldn't see each other every night.*

Of course, that left more time for her to think. Winnie was gone, so she was alone with her thoughts and the music on the radio. "*Now is the hour that we must say good-bye,*" Bing Crosby sang. Jeanie ran to the radio and

## Chapter Twelve

switched the station, catching the last part of Harry James singing *Sleepy Time Gal*.

That was better!

When it ended, there was Guy Lombardo with *"We'll meet again, don't know where, don't know when...."* Jeanie turned off the radio. She took a walk around the block and went to bed.

Kenny came over Wednesday evening, tired as he was, and stretched out on the day bed on the back porch. He told Jeanie a little about his job, but before long he was asleep.

For a moment Jeanie was disappointed. But then, sitting next to him, she began to rock contentedly. It was enough just to be near him. She studied his peaceful face, resisting the urge to smooth back the wavy brown hair that clung damp on his forehead. Surely, he would never be bald. She longed to run her finger down his straight nose, over his heavy eyebrows; but she didn't want to wake him.

She smiled. At least she knew he didn't snore.

At nine o'clock she tenderly kissed him.

He woke with a start, then grabbed her and kissed her until, breathless, she pulled away. "You'd better go home. It's after nine and you have to get up early."

At the door it was more painful then ever to say goodbye, but later she told the sudsy-faced girl in the bathroom mirror that someday they would never have to say good-bye.

Thursday morning, just as Tuesday and Wednesday, the blinds were still drawn on the windows of the special little apartment. Each day Jeanie wondered briefly what had happened but knew that her curiosity was futile. She would never know.

Friday, she had more time to herself at work than

usual because she was running out an order and had less spools to care for. She pulled her little stool next to a post so she could lean back on it, and took out her notebook. Carefully, she went over the figures again. New furniture, even the few essential pieces, would cost more than they could save. Kenny said he wouldn't consider paying for furniture on time.

At noon, she borrowed Marge's newspaper, explaining that she had a little extra time today.

There were few apartments for rent, she discovered, anywhere near her work or a streetcar line. She was about to fold the paper when she saw "Furnished Apartments." She hadn't even thought about a furnished apartment! *Why we wouldn't need to buy any furniture!*

On and on her thoughts went that afternoon and evening. On the way home, as she passed the drawn blinds on the basement apartment, she drew the blinds on her own little living room with its red mahogany furniture. *After all*, she asked herself, *what's new furniture compared to being together?* As much as she wanted to start out in an attractive apartment, being able to get married and be together was really all that mattered.

But, dreams die hard and several times that evening she found herself feeling a bit sad about bidding that cozy living room good-bye—for now.

Saturday evening, Winnie's mother was delighted to hear about Kenny's job. "I really do want to see it work out for you two," she said kindly. She suggested that Kenny come for dinner the next day, but added that she would appreciate it if he would also cut the grass.

Monday night Kenny was grinning when Jeanie opened the door. "Things are really looking good. They hired a whole bunch of new guys today. I suppose we could start making some plans...."

## Chapter Twelve

Jeanie let out a whoop and ran for a calendar.

---

As soon as Emma opened Ella's porch door, she could smell bread baking.

"You must have got an early start," she told her daughter as she hung her purse on the deer antlers by the door.

Ella hurried toward her, wiping her hands on her apron. "It's going to be another hot day, I'm afraid. You said you had some news!" she shouted in Emma's right ear.

"I'll let you read it for yourself." Emma dug in her purse, pulled out Jeanie's letter and handed it to Ella.

Ella motioned for her mother to sit down by the window. She sat down, too, shook the letter open and quickly read it.

Emma held her breath, watching her face as she read. When Ella nodded and smiled she breathed easy again.

Ella leaned closer and shouted. "That's good! It's time they get married. I know they're young, but they'll be all right."

Misty-eyed, Emma agreed. "I'm afraid some people won't think so, but I know those two. They're right for each other."

"September twenty-sixth!" Ella shouted. "That's only a few weeks away. I'm glad she's coming home a week before the wedding."

"I feel so helpless," Emma said, lifting her glasses to dab her eyes. "I just have to leave things to the young folks and help where I can. I'm so glad she is willing to have a cake and ice cream reception right at home. Helen sure isn't up to having a big dinner and no one has the money to hire it done."

Ella nodded. "People will understand."

By afternoon, the fragrance of baking bread was replaced by that of vinegar and pickling spices simmering on the stove.

Mother and daughter sat on the porch slicing cucumbers for bread and butter pickles, as they had more times than they could count.

"Remember the day when Kenny rode out on his bike to see Jeanie and they hiked over here through the woods?" Ella shouted.

Emma smiled and nodded. "Just children. They were fifteen that summer. My land! I never dreamed that day that in three years they would be getting married." She put down the paring knife and rubbed her fingers. "I always enjoyed seeing them together, even way back then. Maybe it was because they were never mean to each other. I can't remember ever seeing them angry at each other. That's unusual."

Ella agreed with a nod.

When Ella went into the kitchen to tend to her pickles, Emma's thoughts went back to that day. It was the second time that summer Kenny had pedaled his bicycle the fourteen miles to see Jeanie. *I forgot that he was coming and promised Ella I would help her can pickles, just like we're doing today. I told Jeanie she'd just have to cook dinner for him. I wasn't a bit worried leaving them alone. But then, when Ella called to invite them over for supper and Helen said they were on their way over through the woods, I was worried. Even though it was only a mile straight through, no one had used that path for years so it was grown up with brush. They didn't come and didn't come....*

Ella came back and picked up her paring knife.

"I was thinking about that day I left the two of them alone and they hiked over here through the woods. At the

## Chapter Twelve

supper table, I saw everyone laughing and didn't know what it was all about until you explained that they had crossed the same fence three times." She laughed. "No wonder it took them so long!"

Ella laughed.

Emma's face grew troubled. "If only it wasn't wartime. It will be so hard for Jeanie if Kenny has to leave her."

Ella leaned closer. "No worse married than single!"

Emma sighed. "That's what I think, too. And Jeanie would have a place to call her own instead of living with other people; a place for Kenny to come back to."

Then, with great effort, Emma listened to news Ella had of the many grandsons who were now in service. She couldn't begin to remember where they all were, but she certainly wanted to hear about them. Being farmers, none of Ella's boys had gone, so far. If any of them went, it would probably be Harold who worked in Lake Geneva. But surely, it wouldn't come to the point where they had to draft young fathers.

When Henry brought in the mail, Emma read the headlines of the newspaper out loud: "Twelve U.S. bombers raid France." She shook her head. "Oh, those poor French people."

Back slicing cucumbers, the conversation drifted back to the wedding plans.

"I don't think Grace will be able to stand up for Jeanie's wedding. She can't miss school."

"Yes, that's too bad. Those three—Jeanie, Grace and Ruby—were always together. I hope she gets a good job when she gets out of business school," Emma said. "I'm glad Ruby is right here. The friend, Pearl, is a nice little girl." Emma chuckled. "But wait till you see her boyfriend, Bud, next to Kenny. He must be at least a foot taller."

Emma continued her monologue. It was easier to talk than to listen. "I sure hope they have good weather. I remember how worried I was before your wedding."

Ella nodded and smiled. "I'm trying to picture little Jeanie a bride; a married woman!"

# 13

As she walked to the Logan Department Store, Jeanie still found it hard to believe how fast things were moving since that night. Sitting beside Kenny on the day bed, she had tentatively circled September 26 on her calendar. They would be married in the little, white country church she had attended from the time she was born.

She was surprised at how fast the letters had come back from Pastor Zaremba and Aunt Helen. Pastor Zaremba must have written immediately to tell them that September twenty-sixth was fine with him.

Helen wrote that she and Roy had talked about giving her a simple reception whenever she got married. But, since the baby was due the first part of November, she would need some help. Helen had added, "Are you sure you want to get married now and then have to be alone if Kenny goes off to war?"

Turning into the department store, Jeanie still felt a bit indignant over Helen's question.

When she had read it to Winnie she said, "How can she be so sure Kenny's going to be drafted?"

Winnie merely stared out the window, not saying a word.

"You think he's going to be drafted, too!" Jeanie accused her.

Winnie shrugged. "Who knows," was all the assurance she had offered.

*But, they're wrong*, Jeanie told herself, determinedly heading for the fabric department.

She still planned to use the sun dress pattern for the bodice of her wedding dress and another pattern for the skirt and train.

After she found the second pattern, she checked the required yardage. Almost seven yards! She did some quick figuring. Her figures told her she could not afford that many yards of even the least expensive satin. Choking back disappointment, she walked from table to table hoping to find some alternative. Ah! There it was! Net! Part of the dress could be rayon net!

Back at the satin table, she lovingly fingered the heaviest fabric. No, she would still have to settle for the cheaper satin. Anyway, she reasoned, it would look almost the same; and, after all, she would only be wearing the dress once.

"I have only fifteen dollars," she told the smiling saleslady as she showed her the pattern.

Her smile vanished. "Oh, dear," she said. "I hope that doesn't include a veil and headpiece."

"Oh, yes!" Jeanie nodded, undaunted. "I've been experimenting and I plan to use pleated net for a headpiece." She demonstrated with a scrap of net. "See, I can

## Chapter Thirteen

fold a three-inch wide piece and pleat it with little box pleats, like this, and sew it as I pleat it. I'd use that for the headpiece and all around the veil. And I want to put it here on the gown for a sweetheart neckline, and around the hipline."

The saleslady studied the pattern. "Hipline?"

Jeanie explained, "I'm going to combine this pattern with another that has a long torso. I need this one for the train."

"My goodness!" the woman said, rolling out yards of the shiny, white satin. "You *are* a smart one!"

Her bill came to fifteen dollars and sixty-one cents. She had to use almost her last penny.

Carrying her precious package, Jeanie didn't care who heard her singing as she walked back to Whipple street.

Jeanie was dying to tell Kenny about her dress, but decided she must keep her excitement to herself. Surely, he would think it was beautiful when it was finished, but would not care to hear all the details.

"I suppose I have to get you a ring?" he said teasingly the next time he came over.

"And what about you? Don't you want a ring?"

"Naw. I've seen too many guys get their rings caught on machinery. Besides, rings are for women."

Jeanie tried not to show her disappointment. She had hoped Kenny would want the whole world to know he was married.

As eager as she was to begin work on her wedding gown, she decided to wait until Saturday. Harry had already told them there would be no work the Saturday of Labor Day weekend. Winnie and her mother would be away at their friend's cottage all weekend and she told Kenny not to come over until evening.

Saturday morning she washed the kitchen floor,

moved the table out of the way and spread the glistening satin on the clean floor.

In a world of white net and satin, she blissfully cut and cut while the radio played love songs. *"Tea for two and two for tea...,"* she sang, and when it came to *"we will raise a family, a girl for you, a boy for me"* she thought of what fun they had had, in their care-free days, talking about the children they would have—eventually. They had even decided on names for two of them; "Kent" for a boy and "Joanie" for a girl. *We haven't talked about them all summer. Too many problems!*

But now, she couldn't remember when she had been so happy.

When she finished the neckline, she held it up and looked in the mirror. She draped the unfinished veil over her head and caught her breath. She actually looked like a *bride!* She closed her eyes and imagined Kenny watching her come down the aisle. What a moment that would be!

"You gonna' work on your dress tomorrow?" Kenny asked that evening.

"Of course not! It's Sunday!"

"Well, you have to get it done!"

"I'll get it done. I have all day Monday."

"Vi said we should come over after church. I think she wants to hear more about our plans."

On the way to Vi's the next day, Jeanie said, "Wouldn't Merle Ann be cute for a flower girl? She has the dress she wore for her aunt Myrtle's wedding in June."

"She'd be cute, all right, but how would that work out? You know Vi and Art can't come, and you plan to go up home a week before the wedding."

"You could bring her with you that Friday night."

"I suppose I could. Think Art and Vi would let her go?"

## Chapter Thirteen

Jeanie shrugged. "We can ask."

They had barely arrived when Kenny's sister said, "You two are up to something. Let's have it!"

Jeanie and Kenny exchanged glances and Kenny said, "You ask her."

"Well," said Jeanie, "we were wondering if Merle Ann could be our flower girl. She did so well at her aunt's wedding and she has that pretty dress."

Vi looked puzzled. "How would that work out? You know Art and I won't be able to be there."

They told her their plan and when Art came home, he said it was fine with him.

That evening, Kenny took Jeanie home instead of going in the opposite direction. As soon as they were in the house he said, "Baby, I can't stay away from you all the time!" and kissed her hungrily.

It was more difficult than ever to say good-bye that night.

By Labor Day evening, Jeanie's wedding gown was finished except for yards of hand-hemming. When Winnie and her mother came home they could hardly believe their eyes.

Jeanie basked in their compliments. "I'll pin my mother's cameo here." She pointed to the center of the sweetheart neckline. "It's pale pink and white."

"How nice to use something of your mother's," Mrs. Janovic said.

At work Tuesday, Eva and Marge plied her with questions about her plans and her dress.

"Have you ordered invitations?" Marge asked.

Jeanie shook her head. "We can't afford them and, anyway, there isn't time. The whole family knows everyone is invited and I'll make some phone calls to friends when I get up there."

"Oh, I wish I could be there," Marge said longingly.

"Me, too," said Eva, but I might be back in Iowa by then."

On the way back to their machines, Jeanie sympathetically squeezed Eva's hand.

"Thanks," Eva said, and turned quickly to her work.

That night on the streetcar, several people actually *smiled* at Jeanie; something rare for Chicago people. *My happiness must show*, she thought, and smiled back.

# 14

It was another of those God's-in-His-heaven-all's-right-with-the-world evenings. Even though the blazing August sun had turned many of the tiny lawns from lush green to dry brown, white and pink petunias still thrived. Jeanie turned her face into the light breeze and hummed contentedly on her way home from work.

She wondered if there would be any letters from home. Though she knew Gram was pleased about their wedding plans, they still hadn't heard from Kenny's parents.

"Maybe we should have written your folks first," she had wondered aloud last night.

Kenny had waved her concern aside. "Naw, they don't have to do anything but come to the wedding, except sign for me." He would be nineteen three days after the wedding.

"But, what if they won't sign?"

"Are you kidding?"

She gave him an acknowledging smile. His parents, especially his mother, had treated her like a daughter for the past two years. It wouldn't make sense for them to suddenly object to their marriage.

When she got home there *was* a letter from Kenny's mother. And, though she was eager to read it, she took a long drink of cool water and settled herself in the back porch rocker before she tore open the envelope.

Before she finished reading even the first line, her rocking came to an abrupt halt. She read the rest of the letter through a blur of tears:

*You kids can't get married the twenty-sixth. Of all times to pick. My sister Frieda's baby is due that week and I promised to help her; and besides, you kids don't have any money! What on earth are you thinking? Kenny hardly got that job. There's too much of this quick marriage business these days. He'll probably go in service and there you'll sit.*

*And for goodness sake, don't go planning a big fancy wedding with a white dress. No one can afford that. Buy a nice gabardine suit you can get some wear out of.*

The letter went on, but it was mostly repetition. However, she didn't say that they wouldn't sign for Kenny. Surely, they knew that would be necessary.

When Winnie came home a few minutes later, Jeanie was crying too hard to talk. She handed her the letter.

"Oh, gosh! That's terrible! And you have so many plans made. What're you gonna' do?"

"I don't know!" Jeanie sobbed

She cried some more in the bathroom, rinsed her face and flopped on her bed. Her nearly-finished wedding gown taunted her from where it hung on the door.

## Chapter Fourteen

Winnie's short hair swung across her face as she leaned over Jeanie. "Come have a bacon, lettuce and tomato sandwich," she urged.

Jeanie shook her head. "I'm not hungry."

Winnie quietly sat down beside her.

"We were going to go and get our blood tests tonight," Jeanie sniffled.

"I know. Remember, I told you where to find our doctor."

Winnie slipped away and came back with a glass of orange juice. "Here, drink this. You know you get weak when you get hungry."

Jeanie gratefully downed it. "Oh, Winnie, I'm glad you're here."

"What in thunder...?" Kenny said when he saw her red eyes. "We gotta get going to the doctor and look at you!"

She handed him the letter.

His eyes sped over the page. He groaned and shook his head. "I should have known! We shoulda' written to them first of all. I think Ma's put out because we made all the plans without her. Dad wouldn't care."

Jeanie groaned. "What are we going to do?"

"I don't know...." He lit a cigarette. "Well, we could go and see what Vi thinks we should do."

Jeanie held back her tears on the streetcar, but she burst into tears when Vi opened the door.

Kenny handed Vi their mother's letter.

Vi took the letter and sat down at the kitchen table. As she read, she caught her breath and bit her bottom lip. "Oh, I should have warned you. Mother hates to be left out of things. She's miffed because she wasn't in on the planning."

"What're we going to do? The Pastor, the couples who are standing up...." Jeanie was crying too hard to go on.

Vi sat with her eyes closed, her fingernails tapping the table top. "I think," she said without opening her eyes, "that Mother already has another letter in the mail." She opened her eyes and smiled reassuringly at Kenny and Jeanie. "She does that. Something upsets her and she sits right down and writes before she even thinks things over. Later, she's sorry." She laughed a wry laugh. "You should have read the letter she wrote when she found out I would have another baby about the time Buddy was a year old."

"Yeah, I know how she is," Kenny agreed. "She goes off like a rocket, but then she's sorry and tries to makeup for it. But, what do we do now?"

Vi quickly stood up. "Go and have those blood tests! Tomorrow is Wednesday and the doctor's office will be closed."

Kenny stared at the floor. "Well...I suppose...."

"Get going!" Vi ordered. "You better hurry! It's after eight."

They ran. Oh! how they ran. Jeanie's legs almost buckled under her when they got to the top of the stairs.

They nearly bumped into the doctor on his way out.

"We're getting married the twenty-sixth and we need our blood tests," Kenny panted.

The doctor smiled indulgently and told Jeanie to come into the examining room.

"Well, we made it just in time," Kenny told Vi when they got back. "Thanks for getting us moving!"

At lunchtime the next day Jeanie sat with a newspaper and a street guide, studying the "For Rent" ads. There weren't many furnished apartments within their price range, she soon discovered.

## Chapter Fourteen

"We want to get something close to a streetcar line and not too far for either of us to get to work," she explained to Eva and Marge.

That night she and Kenny went to look at a furnished apartment near Fullerton Avenue. A lady in a soiled cotton dress opened the door and Jeanie wrinkled her nose as stale cooking odors enveloped them.

After exchanging a questioning glance, they followed her up a steep flight of stairs and down a dingy corridor to a door with a tin number eight on it.

The woman jangled keys until she found the right one and threw open the door.

Jeanie inwardly cringed. The walls were shiny bold green and a sagging curtain separated the bedroom and the all-purpose room.

"All the hot water you want," the woman told them. "no utilities to pay. Just twelve dollars a week."

"Ah...thank you," said Jeanie, without even looking at Kenny. "This isn't quite what we're looking for."

"You won't get anything better for the money," the woman called after them.

Out on the street, Jeanie shuddered.

"I'd pitch a tent before I'd live in that hole," Kenny said.

The next place was on Division Street near California. If it proved to be good, Jeanie wouldn't even have to change streetcars to get to work.

"Well," Kenny said, "let's hope this one is better."

It was a smaller building. The dirty entrance-way made Jeanie want to turn and run.

A man wearing a stained undershirt answered the door and told them he'd meet them in the rear. The tiny backyard was piled with junk.

"I don't even want to look at it," Kenny said, and

when the man opened the back door he told him, "We've changed our minds. Thanks anyway."

Hand in hand, they ran to catch the streetcar.

"Whew!" Kenny said plopping onto the seat. He checked his watch. "Time to quit for tonight."

At work the next day, Jeanie changed spools and prayed they would find a nice, clean place to live. She had been doing a lot of praying lately, but none more earnestly than today. The days were going fast. They simply *had* to find an apartment.

There was another letter from Kenny's mother that night. Anxiously, Jeanie tore it open and read:

*Dear kids.*

*I'm sorry I was upset about your wedding plans. I told Frieda and she said she can get a neighbor to help for a day or two if I can't be there.*

*I'm sorry about what I said about the white dress, too. I remember now that you said it had always been your dream. You certainly will be a pretty bride.*

*We'll go out to the farm and see what we can do to help your aunt and uncle. I'm glad you're coming up a week before the wedding. You'll need to go to Medford for the license and flowers and order a cake. You'll have to make an appointment for pictures, too. I'll take you. Let me know when you want to go.*

*I sure wish Ray and Vi and Art could be there.*

Jeanie breathed a sigh of relief and called Winnie.

After Winnie read the letter, she grabbed Jeanie and they danced around the room.

"I *knew* it would be all right!" she told Jeanie.

Before Jeanie had finished her letter to Kenny's parents,

## Chapter Fourteen

Kenny arrived. "Ask her if she'll take care of Merle Ann."

They mailed the letter and went to see more apartments.

One of them wasn't too bad, but that one was twenty-five dollars a week; more than Jeanie earned. "Too much," Kenny said when Jeanie looked hopeful. "You don't even earn that much a week."

Jeanie felt a chill. Was he implying that she would, someday, be paying for it alone?

The other two apartments were impossible. Holding hands on the streetcar, they barely talked to each other on the way home.

Winnie was sympathetic when they dragged in. "I've been thinking...you could stay here awhile after you're married. I don't think my mother would mind." She laughed, "Kenny's been here most of the time anyway."

Jeanie was too choked up to talk for a moment. This girl had become a true friend. "Thanks, Winnie," she said quietly, "but we'll find something."

In bed that night, she wondered if a good furnished apartment within their price range actually existed. She had been willing to give up her dream of using their own furniture, but that was before she had seen how ugly those furnished places could be.

Friday night they went to see one at 3718 Concord Place, a street that was not even a block long because the railroad track cut if off on the west end.

The houses were close together like Mozart street, but they were all one-family houses. "It's probably an attic," Kenny said.

When they found the place midway down the block, Jeanie noticed there were no scraps of paper or litter of any kind in the tiny yard and the steps looked newly painted. She also saw neat white curtains hanging at the front window.

A gaunt elderly man answered the door and a tiny old lady peered from behind him.

"Ah...we're getting married soon and we saw your ad," Kenny said. "Is the apartment still for rent?"

The old man studied them for a moment before he spoke. "Kinda' young to be getting married, aren't ya'?"

Jeanie felt her cheeks flush. "We've been going together almost four years. We're from Wisconsin."

"Humph," the man said gruffly. He turned to his wife and she gave him a slight nod. "Come up around the back," he told them.

The passageway was clean, too, and so were the back stairs.

"They're awfully old," Kenny said. "They could die and then where'd we be?"

"They look like a nice couple, though," Jeanie whispered.

The stairs had one landing and then another short flight before they reached a tiny, open porch.

The old man opened the door and offered an arthritic hand. "I'm Mr. Rassmussen."

Kenny shook his hand, introduced himself and Jeanie. They followed him into the kitchen of the apartment.

Jeanie winced at the ugly, dark-brown wainscoting behind the double drainboard sink. A black, four-burner gas stove stood to the right of the door leading to the front room. A plain brown wooden table with four chairs stood in the center of the room, and there was an old wooden icebox on the wall opposite the sink.

"You can hang lots of clothes in this," the old man said, opening a small wardrobe built into a corner.

They nodded. "And here," he opened a dwarf-sized door to the left of the back entrance, "is the pantry." There were shelves and a tiny window, but one had to crouch

## Chapter Fourteen

down to get into it. The shelves, Jeanie noted, held an assortment of old dishes.

"I'm going to paint this," the old man said, tapping his finger on a porcelain-topped cabinet that stood next to the sink. It had worn spots around the drawer and door handles.

He then led them into the front room.

*They certainly must like black*, Jeanie thought. Two rockers and two chairs with arms, as well as two lamp tables, were all painted black. The only items of varnished wood were a dresser with a cloudy mirror and a chest of drawers. The bed frame was brown metal. A maroon oriental design rug covered most of the floor and limp, white curtains hung at the double windows at end of the combination living room and bedroom.

"Lots of room for storage here," the old man announced, opening another door with under-the-eaves space similar to the pantry.

Jeanie was not impressed.

"The bathroom is there," he pointed. It was up one step and to the right of the door between the two rooms.

*Not bad!* Jeanie thought. The sink and bathtub were small but spotless. There was a nice window showing a bit of the roof next door, but mostly sky.

Back in the kitchen, the old man told them the previous tenants had just moved out and he wanted to do some cleaning before he rented it again. "But, it should be ready by the nineteenth."

Jeanie squeezed Kenny's hand and he pulled her into the front room. "What do you think?"

Jeanie sighed. "It's not the greatest but it sure beats what we've seen so far. The ad said seven dollars a week. Let's ask him for sure."

"Ah...the ad said seven dollars a week," Kenny said. "That right?"

The old man simply nodded.

"We'd like to take it. Jeanie's going to go up home early to get ready for the wedding on the twenty-sixth, but I'd like to move in as soon as it's ready. I've been living at a YMCA."

The old man looked deep into Kenny's eyes and then into Jeanie's. "Your folks givin' you any trouble about getting married?"

"Oh, no!" they both assured him.

He still seemed doubtful. "I just don't want someone comin' here and hauling off this young lady in a week or so 'cause they didn't approve."

Jeanie laughed. "You don't have to worry about that!"

"All right then," he finally agreed. "Give me seven dollars and it's yours on the nineteenth."

When Kenny gave him the money he pulled a receipt book out of his back pocket and, holding a pen between knobby fingers, painstakingly wrote it out.

"There now." He smiled at them for the first time. "We'll have it nice and clean for you.

On the streetcar, they decided to go over and tell Vi. "You sure it's going to be all right?" Kenny asked, searching Jeanie's face. "It's not much of a place."

"I know," she sighed. "Still I feel good about it. The other places gave me the creeps. There's only the old couple and us. Not a whole bunch of strangers under one roof." She cuddled close to him. "Just think! It will be *ours!*"

By the time they got to Vi's, they were both feeling enthusiastic about it.

"I'll take the mirror off the dresser and hide it in the storage space. It's pretty bad," Jeanie told Vi. "And if we

## Chapter Fourteen

push the bed way in the corner it will look more like a living room."

"Does it have good windows?" Vi asked.

Jeanie wrinkled her nose. "The woodwork is pretty bad, but the front windows are fairly good-sized. The only window in the kitchen is the one in the door."

"You aren't too thrilled about it, are you?" Vi said.

Jeanie shrugged. "No, but it will do for awhile. It should be quiet with just the two old people downstairs."

Next day at work, Jeanie told the girls, "We found a little attic apartment last night. It's not so great, but I think we're going to be able to make it real cozy," she said bravely.

But, at her machines, Jeanie tried to convince herself they could make that plain, little attic into a cozy home.

# 15

Day after day, wedding plans occupied Jeanie's thoughts at work and her little notebook was soon filled with details.

"I think I have things pretty well planned," she told Kenny, "But of course there are a lot of things Helen and I will have to decide together."

"Yeah, but one thing we haven't done anything about is the wedding dance."

"Wedding dance!" Jeanie groaned. "I hate those smelly, old dance halls! Do we *have* to have one?"

"Sure we do. That's the only chance we'll have to see our friends. We can't invite everyone to the reception."

"Oh, I suppose we have to."

"Ah, honey! It'll be fun. Remember your cousin Myrtle's wedding dance? You were so thrilled when we watched them dance alone and then the whole wedding party came on the floor and everyone clapped."

## Chapter Fifteen

Jeanie nodded.

"Oh, baby! You're going to be the most beautiful bride! I want everyone to see you!"

"Oh...all right."

"I'll write to my folks. They're good friends with Al and Hulda at the Lakeside. If they don't have another wedding dance scheduled, I know we can have it there. They'll get a band—we have to pay for that— and the hall's free."

"Another thing we have to ask your folks to do! And you said they didn't have to do anything but sign for you. I'm glad your mother offered to drive me to Medford to order the flowers and cake and everything. Roy is always so busy."

"Yeah, I sure wish I could go up there and we could do it all together, but I can't take a week off now if I want to keep my job."

"I know...I still feel scared when I think about dancing at our wedding dance."

Kenny gathered her close. "It'll be fun, you'll see! Just think how it will be: you in your wedding gown; just the two of us dancing to *I Love You Truly*. Then, the rest of the wedding party will join in and, after that, all the guys will try to dance with the bride."

"That's the part that really scares me. You know I can't dance."

Kenny laughed. "Don't worry about that! The floor will be so full no one can move anyway!"

Again, that night before she went to sleep, Jeanie tried to think of ways to make their apartment look better. She choked back disappointment when she thought of the grooved wood wainscoting which, for some unknown reason, she had hated ever since she was a little girl. Maybe she could cover it with some bright oilcloth. That old brown table looked awful, too, but that she could cover with her embroidered tablecloths.

She had to part with her dreams of a honeymoon, a cozy apartment and new furniture; but those things had not been within her control. She smiled into the darkness. There was still one dream that was within her control!

She saw herself gliding down the aisle in her white satin and net gown; and Kenny watching her with his blue eyes so full of love that she'd be aware of nothing else.

It didn't matter what anyone else would think that day. The two of them would know they were starting their marriage right.

---

A heat wave the next few days became more bearable as Jeanie concentrated on the wedding. She could see blonde-haired Ruby in her powder-blue gown and Pearl in pale pink with her ever-perfect, dark brown "page boy." Or, had she, perhaps, changed her hair style since May?

Oh, it would be fun to be with all the aunts, uncles and cousins out on the lawn under the box-elder trees. As always, the porch swing would be constantly occupied and Gram would walk around nodding and smiling as if she really knew what was being said. There would be all those good wishes and advice from well-meaning dear ones. The little girls would stare at her billowing gown, dreaming about their own weddings, and little boys would duck their head in embarrassment whenever Kenny kissed her.

And then they'd be together, alone.

Jeanie came back down to earth long enough to hoist another rack of spools onto the stack at the end of one

## Chapter Fifteen

machine. Right now, thoughts of problems seemed far away. It must be Gram's prayers, she decided. She thought of the evenings back home when she was in high school. Gram would go to bed and Jeanie would cover her ears, not wanting to hear Gram's loudly whispered prayers.

"All things work together for good to them that love God, to them who are called according to his purpose," Gram often reminded her those days.

It sounded wonderful, but Jeanie still had her doubts. First of all, she wasn't at all sure she was "called according to his purpose," Second, she didn't really *feel* love for God.

*Oh, I want to love God. But how can a person love Him when He's so far away? It seems like He's always frowning at me.* She sighed. *Maybe when I get old like Gram and don't do so many things wrong, I'll be able to talk to Him like Gram does.*

But, she didn't want to wait that long! *Oh, I want to be closer to You!* she whispered.

Only a few more days and she would be going up home.

At noon, Jeanie bumped into Eva in the washroom doorway and saw that she had been crying. "I won't be here when you get back," Eva said.

When they sat down to eat, Eva said, "I thought I was prepared for Frank's leaving, but I guess I wasn't." Her lunch bag remained unopened as did the two others.

Jeanie leaned over and hugged her. She wanted to tell her how much she would miss her, but there was too big a lump in her throat.

Eva brushed away tears and opened her lunch bag. "Come on, you gals! If we all stop eating every time a guy is drafted, who'll make the parachute cords?"

After lunch, as they headed back to their machines,

Marge gave Jeanie a sympathetic look. "I wish this hadn't happened right now, just before your wedding."

Jeanie nodded. "I have to face the fact that Kenny could be drafted, too, but right now I don't even want to think about it." She turned pleading eyes on Marge, "Is it all right if I'm happy *right now?*"

Marge caught her in a fierce hug. "You bet it is! When the hard times come, you'll need to face them, but right now...." She stepped back and took Jeanie's face in her hands. "Right now, *you just be happy!*"

---

There was trouble, Emma certainly knew that, but she didn't know what. Kenny's parents had come about half an hour ago. They had greeted her pleasantly and Emma understood that they had come to talk with Roy and Helen who were just finishing dinner.

Emma had excused herself because she couldn't hear what was being said, and had gone back to her room to knit and wait. After what seemed like a long time, she had gone to the door. Their loud voices told her something was wrong. When she saw Kenny's mother's dark eyes blazing and Roy and Helen's red faces, she suddenly felt weak.

Now, back in her rocker, she waited and prayed. *Lord, I don't know what's wrong, but I ask you to take care of it. Let me know if there is anything I can do.*

Finally, she could sit still no longer and went to the door again, being careful not to be seen. Again, she heard shouting.

With a weary sigh, she sat down in her rocker. Whatever it was, it was about Jeanie and Kenny.

A shadow passed the east window and Emma got up in time to see their car pull out of the driveway.

*Chapter Fifteen*

When she turned, Roy was standing at the door. He motioned for her to sit down and drew the other rocker close.

"It's all right," he shouted.

Emma watched his face closely and strained to hear.

"They wanted to have beer...here at the house."

Emma frowned. There had been no liquor, that she knew of, at any family gatherings for many years.

"Kenny's folks are going to have a little dinner for the kids in town."

Later, after Roy had gone, Emma thought of dozens of questions. A little later, when she walked through Helen's kitchen with a pail of water from the pump, she saw that Helen was still upset and decided not to question her.

Again, Emma picked up her knitting. Too bad they couldn't have come to some agreement to have the reception here. Jeanie had written several pages about how she wanted the whole family, as well as Kenny's aunts, uncles and cousins to come after the ceremony. Emma shook her head and sighed. She would simply have to wait and see what happened. Meanwhile, she could pray.

Much to Jeanie's disappointment the railroad coach she boarded Friday night was not one of the plush Hiawatha cars with soft, reclining seats. This one had stiff straight seats no more comfortable than on a streetcar. She sniffed disdainfully at the odor of a thousand ancient cigars.

She got a pillow from the conductor, but was unable to sleep as the old coach jolted, squeaked and swayed through dismal rain.

When they changed at New Lisbon, she gratefully

*Satin in the Snow*

allowed a young soldier to carry her suitcase. He tried to make conversation, but she simply thanked him and took the seat in front of him, next to a fat old man.

It proved to be a good choice because the man got off at the next station and Jeanie had the whole seat to herself. For a while she sat up like a "proper" young lady. But, before too long, she did what she saw others doing: stretched out on the empty seat with her coat over her as a blanket.

It was daylight when the train lurched to a stop, but Jeanie couldn't tell what station they were in. Her head ached, her eyes burned and her heart thumped, as it always did when she did not get enough sleep.

She snapped to attention when the conductor marched into the car and shouted, "We've run into a little trouble, folks. There's been a flood and this is as far as we can go!"

"Oh, no!" Jeanie groaned aloud in chorus with other passengers' grumbles and groans.

"Wait a minute," shouted the conductor. "We've called for buses and they'll take you up the line. They might have to take some detours. Lots of bridges are out. But you'll get to your destinations."

*But when?* Jeanie thought in dismay. Kenny's mother was coming at noon to take her to the courthouse in Medford for the marriage license. If they didn't get their license today, maybe they couldn't get married next Saturday.

Tears blinded her as she reached up to haul her heavy suitcase down from the rack.

"Here! Let me get it!" insisted the young soldier behind her.

She tearfully mumbled her thanks.

## Chapter Fifteen

"Hey? What's the matter?" he said, "You're going to get where you're headed."

Jeanie stared out the window. "I know, but maybe not in time. I'm supposed to get our marriage license at Medford today."

The soldier grinned. "Where's the lucky guy?"

"Back in Chicago."

"Here," he patted the seat beside him. "You might as well sit down and tell me all about it. Doesn't look like we'll be going anywhere too soon."

She had just begun to tell him about their wedding plans when the conductor shouted, "The buses are here!"

---

Roy was waiting for Jeanie at Tomahawk. He knew all about the flood and had expected her to be late.

"The bridge across the creek is out but the iron bridge is still holding," he told her as they pulled away in his mud-spattered car.

Gray clouds brooded over the autumn-colored woods. "Not such a pretty drive today," Roy said. "Lots of leaves still nice though." He studied the broken clouds. "Maybe the sun will come this afternoon," he observed.

"The lawn must be a soggy mess," Jeanie said and when Roy didn't answer she added, "Oh, well, it will dry out in a week."

When they reached the road at the county line Roy said, "Can't take this road today. It's flooded all along the river. We'll go up past Semrow's and Lind's. That was really something the way the bridge below the hill washed out last night. Cracked that big concrete arch right in two and pushed her apart a couple feet."

When they reached Larson's hill, just south of Lind's, Jeanie felt a surge of excitement as she looked down on the home-farm half a mile away and the miles of forest beyond. Though clouds muted its colors, it was still a lovely sight.

"Oh, I forgot how far you can see from this hill!" she exclaimed.

"Yup," Roy said. "You can even see the Tomyhawk paper mill smoke on a clear day."

At the corner where they turned east, Jeanie glanced fondly at the little white church where she and Kenny would be married in a week. They sailed down the little hill, across the level stretch and, at the crest of the long slope before the farm, Jeanie hungrily drank in the scene. It was wonderful to see the big, old pine trees; the familiar white house; the big, red barn; and the smaller outbuildings. She thought she caught a glimpse of Gram near the woodshed.

She had been right. When they pulled up by the garage, Gram hurried toward them with her apron filled with sticks and bark.

Jeanie hugged her tight, breathing in the familiar scent of wood smoke on her clothes. Gram hugged her back as best she could without spilling her apron-load of firewood.

"Oh, my goodness, girl, you look tired!" Gram said as she bustled toward the house. "Dinner's ready. You eat first and then you can rest."

Never had Jeanie wished more that Gram could hear well. It wouldn't be easy explaining that Kenny's mother would be here to pick her up in less than an hour.

"Well...at least you didn't have to swim!" Helen chuckled when Jeanie walked into her kitchen. "Did you look down toward the river?"

*Chapter Fifteen*

Jeanie shook her head, feeling somewhat dazed.

Marilyn ran in, wearing her same old, faded, red baseball cap. Jeanie snatched it off. "Just wanted to see if you still had hair under there!"

Marilyn giggled.

Jeanie swooped chubby little Arne up and hugged him.

"You're heavy!"

He nodded seriously. "I growed."

Shy, little Marie stood by letting her smile and her warm, brown eyes speak for her.

Ronny looked as if he had grown an inch a month. "Let me know if you need some help," he called over his shoulder on his way upstairs with her suitcase.

It was good to be home!

"Oh, we have a lot of planning to do," Jeanie said to Helen, who was setting her own big table. "But Gram wants me to come and eat now."

Helen avoided Jeanie's eyes. "Well...actually, we don't have anything to plan. You need to talk to Kenny's mother."

Jeanie's knees felt weak and she clutched the back of a chair. She didn't like the tone of Helen's voice at all.

"What do you mean *I have to talk to her*?"

Helen's face was immobile. "She'll tell you. She's taking over the whole thing."

Roy came in looking grim and Jeanie could see that Helen was close to tears. "Yeah, I didn't want to tell you till we got home," he said. "They came out here the other day and insisted that there had to be beer, and that there should be a dinner instead of just cake and ice cream like we had planned." He rolled up his sleeves to wash his hands for dinner. "We told 'em we don't have liquor on this place and we can't manage a big dinner right now."

*Satin in the Snow*

Watching Helen waddle to the pantry, and noting her swollen ankles, Jeanie understood what Roy meant. Helen had written that the baby was due about the first of November.

Roy began to wash his hands and Helen stayed in the pantry. Jeanie retreated to Gram's room on shaky legs. Now she *really* wished Gram could hear.

Gram saw her stricken face and patted her arm. "I don't know what to make of it all," she said in her none-too-quiet whisper. She shook her head. "There was a lot of loud talking and I could see everyone was awfully upset. Roy told me Kenny's folks are taking care of the reception, that's all I know. I think they're feeling real bad."

Jeanie was about to cry when Gram shook her finger at her. "Now, none of that! Things will work out. You just think about the two of you being together and don't you mind all the rest. The wedding is only one day, but your marriage is for your lifetime!"

Ronnie poked his head around their doorway, "Jeanie! Telephone!"

It was Kenny's mother, talking very loud and fast. "I can't get through to pick you up, but I called the courthouse and you can get the license Monday and still be in time, they told me."

"Oh, thank heaven!" Jeanie exclaimed. "I was so worried."

"Did your aunt and uncle tell you about the change in plans for the reception?"

"Ah...yes...but, I..."

"Now, don't you worry about a thing! We'll have a little dinner here at Nettie's. She owes me a few favors. We'll invite the wedding party and the Pastor and his wife and your grandma and your uncle and aunt."

"But, I wanted...."

## Chapter Fifteen

"There isn't a thing for you to do but be there! The week will go fast enough for you. I've hired a couple of girls to serve and the rest is all taken care of. Things are all set for the wedding dance at Lakeside, too. You can go to Medford for the pictures right after the ceremony, come back to Nettie's for dinner and then go right over to the dance," she rushed on. "Of course, I'll take care of Merle Ann, too, and pick her and Kenny up from the train Saturday morning. She *is* coming, isn't she?"

"As far as I know," Jeanie answered weakly.

"Well, you just rest today and I'll see you about nine Monday morning. We'll have a lot to do!"

Back in Gram's room Jeanie snatched a scrap of paper and a pencil and quickly wrote what Kenny's mother had told her and handed it to her grandmother.

She read it slowly, glancing up at Jeanie now and then. When she finished she sighed and handed the note back.

"That wasn't what you wanted at all, was it?" she said, her brow furrowed.

Jeanie gulped back tears.

"Like I said before," Gram continued, holding Jeanie's eyes. "Think about what's important and don't let all this wedding business get you down." She peered at Jeanie over the rims of her glasses. "You be careful what you write to Kenny about all this. There are hard feelings enough!"

For a moment their eyes held and Jeanie noticed that Gram's lids had drooped even more. An intricate network of lines surrounded them. But those gray-blue eyes still had a way of looking right into a person's soul. Though she couldn't contribute money, or even work, she was still in charge in her own wise way. Jeanie forced a smile and nodded. She even managed to eat a little dinner.

"You better go upstairs and sleep awhile," Gram told

her when they had finished eating. "Things always seem worse when a person's tired."

Jeanie nodded and staggered upstairs to her old room.

She flopped down on her familiar and comforting bed. What else could happen? Too tired to even cry, she groaned and rolled over into the pillow that smelled like fresh air. If only Kenny was here and they could talk it all over!

She gave a wry laugh. What was there to talk over? Arrangements had been totally taken out of her hands.

# 16

After church service Sunday morning, Pastor Zaremba beamed a reassuring smile at Jeanie before telling her he had scheduled the wedding rehearsal on Friday evening. "You can tell Kenny whatever he needs to know. I'm sure he'll do just fine."

Another disappointment! Had she ever dreamed her wedding rehearsal would take place without the groom? It had to, of course, because Kenny's boss at Dryden Rubber Company was reluctant to let him take off even Saturday. He would have to catch the train Friday night in order to be on time for the wedding Saturday afternoon.

Jeanie invited Ruby to come home with them after church. "I'm going to sort out my linens and pack them in the big wooden box my mother used for her school supplies. Want to help me?"

Gram's eyes twinkled as she watched, more than heard, the girls laughing and talking at lunchtime.

After they had eaten, they ran up to Jeanie's room to sort and pack Jeanie's linens in the hope chest. "Roy is going to take it to the freight office for me," Jeanie said.

On their knees in front of the cedar chest, Jeanie laid aside her mother's wedding nightgown—white cotton muslin with modest long sleeves and a crocheted inset at the neck.

"You're not going to wear it?" Ruby teased.

"Oh, you...want to see what I *am* going to wear?"

Ruby nodded and Jeanie sprang up and took a filmy, pink gown with narrow satin straps from her suitcase. "I think Kenny will like this one better."

Back in front of the cedar chest, Jeanie lifted out a pile of linens and sat back on her heels. "I sure didn't think we'd be spending our first night right here. We had planned to take a hotel room in Tomahawk, but then we thought about all the driving Bud would have to do and changed our minds. Besides, if we stayed there I wouldn't get to say good-bye to Gram or anyone, and then, we'll have Merle Ann going back with us...." She sighed. "It was just too complicated. We'll come home after the dance and stay here." She handed Ruby a stack of flour-sack dishtowels with a day-of-the-week design embroidered on each one.

"Oh, I remember when you were working on these," Ruby said as if eager to change the subject. "Now, for goodness sakes don't use 'Wednesday' on Friday, or 'Tuesday' on Sunday!" she teased.

Jeanie laughed "It's really a dumb idea, but I had fun embroidering them."

"And now you'll get to use them," Ruby said fondly.

Jeanie nodded. It was hard to know what to say—

## Chapter Sixteen

knowing Ruby's fiancé, Chet, had already been in service many months and they had no idea when he would be home. She handed her cousin a neat stack of sheets and pillowcases.

"Three sets! Are you lucky!" Ruby marveled. "The way things are going with the war, before long we won't be able to buy any linens, not even towels."

"I've only got two hand towels and a bath towel. I hope I can find a couple more."

"You'll probably get some at your shower. You *do* know we're having a shower for you on Wednesday?"

Jeanie shook her head. "No one told me, but I thought maybe there would be one."

"I'm sure Helen would have told you by tomorrow. We decided not to try to make it a surprise because it will be right here."

Jeanie sat back on the floor hugging her knees. "I'm pleased, but I'm kinda scared too...all those ladies looking at me. I hope I do everything right. You'll help me open gifts, won't you?"

"Of course! Won't that be fun?"

"Oh, I almost forgot to tell you, Helen said I should invite the wedding party over for cake after the rehearsal Friday evening. I think she feels bad about...."

"We all do," Ruby interrupted. "It's just a shame."

They were both silent a moment, not wanting to say anything they might later regret. When Jeanie suddenly chuckled, Ruby seemed surprised.

"I was just remembering how you and I and Grace used to talk about the house we'd have when we grew up; how many bathrooms and bedrooms it would have...."

Ruby laughed. "And how many servants!"

"And now," Jeanie said wistfully, "we don't have money for even simple things. What a difference money would make. We could pay for our own reception and invite everyone we wanted." She caught Ruby's eyes. "I hope I get a chance to tell your folks how sorry I am that I can't invite them to the dinner."

Ruby waved away Jeanie's concern. "They know. Everyone understands with Helen's baby due so soon and all."

Jeanie dug into the chest and held out an assortment of doilies, potholders and washcloths. "I never dreamed so many things could go wrong or that I'd have to settle for so many things I don't like. Our apartment is just two, little attic rooms full of ugly, old furniture and our honeymoon will be the train ride back to Chicago—with Merle Ann!"

"At least you'll be together," Ruby said softly.

Jeanie felt her face flush. How could she complain about such trivial things when Ruby and Chet, and so many other young couples, didn't know when or if they would see each other again!

That evening Jeanie began a letter to Kenny, tore it up and started another one. How could she tell him about the hard feelings between the families without seeming to take sides herself?

She decided not to mention the reception at all. It really didn't matter that much to him anyway. What he was looking forward to was seeing all his friends at the wedding dance.

She wrote about the flood and her trouble getting home; about the plans for the rehearsal; and how she would tell him all he would need to know when he brought the flowers out Saturday forenoon. Of course, she also told him how much she missed him.

Monday morning, Kenny's mother was all smiles when she came to get her. Jeanie tried to smile, too. But

## Chapter Sixteen

on the way to Medford, the conversation became so uncomfortable that Jeanie had all she could do to hold her tongue. She could see both sides. Kenny's family drank beer as casually as her family drank lemonade; while her family, because of sad experiences many years ago with those who drank too much, considered all alcoholic drinks a curse and liquor was no longer brought to the homestead. How many times, Jeanie wondered, had she heard Gram say, "If it wasn't for that first drink, there would be no drunkards!" She wasn't about to be responsible for anyone having that first drink at *her* house.

However, Kenny's mother seemed oblivious to Jeanie's discomfort and chattered on. "Now, don't worry about the reception. Like I said, Nettie owes me some favors and it won't cost you kids a thing. You have enough expenses. And everything's set for the wedding dance, too, but we do have to stop at Dake studio and make an appointment for the photographs."

Jeanie felt as if she were being swept down a swiftly-flowing stream.

At the florist, she studied all the pictures of bridesmaid's bouquets and chose a nosegay of tiny pink roses for Merle Ann, and wrist corsages of pink and white carnations for Ruby and Pearl. When it came to choosing her own bouquet, Jeanie lingered over an old-fashioned one with ribbon streamers like the one she had seen in Gram's old photo album. She shook her head. "That's too expensive!" she said and turned the page.

They looked at several others before Kenny's mother said, "You really like the one with the ribbon streamers, don't you? I think Kenny would want you to have that one. After all," she added, "it's *your* wedding. You should have what you want!"

The irony of that statement caught Jeanie off guard.

She quickly choked back a sarcastic response. *Is this the same woman who hasn't been paying one bit of attention to what I wanted?*

She had an impulse to choose another bouquet just to show the older lady she would make her own decision; but decided she did want the one with streamers and ordered it.

At the bakery, Jeanie said, "I want it all white." The sales lady explained that if the bride and groom ornament for the top was returned, there would be no charge. Kenny's mother volunteered to return it. As it was, the three-tiered cake would cost three dollars.

It was difficult to stay angry at someone who was willing to do so much for them. *I'll just have to take her the way she is, the bitter with the sweet!*

Gram looked worried when Jeanie walked in. "Everything go all right?" she asked, moving a pot of chicken soup over to the front stove lid.

Jeanie nodded and scribbled, "We got everything taken care of, but I'm tired!"

"I bet you *are* tired," Gram said sympathetically. "Tension can make a person more tired than hard work."

Jeanie caught Gram's eye and nodded.

Over the hearty, welcome soup, Jeanie relaxed a bit.

"I sure wish I could do more to help," Gram said. "You just let me know if there is *anything* I can do."

That evening Jeanie walked through the dewy grass and breathed the cool, sweet air, thinking of the contrast between it and the hot, heavy air of Heinemann's. How many city people, Jeanie wondered, had ever seen the starry sky in complete darkness. Even in a few months, she had forgotten the myriads of stars because only the brightest ones could be seen in the light-reflecting city sky.

## Chapter Sixteen

"The heavens declare the glory of God...." she whispered as she gazed upward until her neck began to hurt. She shivered and wrapped her arms around herself, feeling infinitely tiny and insignificant. How could Gram dare to pray on and on to this great Ruler of the universe?

She had gone into the house without attempting to pray, but with a heightened yearning to know God as Gram did.

When she came in, Gram looked up with that endearing combination of a nod, a smile and a wink and Jeanie flashed her a warm smile.

Often these days, Jeanie would glance up and find Gram looking at her with love in her eyes that she had never seen before. *Maybe it's because I'm learning to be more loving,* she thought.

What's more, Gram hadn't scolded at all! She talked about what other family members were doing, where the grandsons were stationed and now and then about some amusing incident. All Jeanie had to do was nod and smile.

At times, when Gram wasn't aware of it, Jeanie studied her calm features. Of course, she was more wrinkled than ever, but there were none of the harsh frown lines that made some old ladies look so dour. There was also a dignity about her, even in the midst of her worn furniture and jumble of designs and colors. Jeanie closed her eyes and imagined Gram seated in an elegant color-coordinated room. She was wearing that same tranquil expression. Surroundings, Jeanie realized, would not change Gram. The peace she exuded came from within.

*Some day...someday, I'll look like that,* Jeanie promised herself.

# 17

"So you and Kenny's mother got everything taken care of in Medford yesterday," Olga said.

Jeanie watched her aunt put wood in the pale green and ivory cook stove. "Yes, things are all set." She chuckled. "Now, all we need is the groom. He'll be coming on the train, Friday night."

Jeanie strolled across the living room and looked through the window at the empty log house she had watched Carl and Roy build over ten years ago. Jeanie was glad Carl and Olga were living in the new, much larger, frame house; but it saddened her to see the bare windows of the house that held so many good memories. She sat down in Carl's rocker while Olga folded clothes fresh from the clothesline. They reminisced about the many hours she had spent with them in that little house; about the time she dropped Olga's only sewing needle down a

*Chapter Seventeen*

crack in the floor; how she had beaten a pan of fudge over the water pail and couldn't understand why it wouldn't get thick, until Olga saw water splashing into it; and the time she carried laundry out to the clothesline on newspaper, which soaked through. The clean clothes fell in the mud and had to be rewashed.

Jeanie groaned. "How did you ever put up with me?"

"Oh, we managed," Olga said teasingly.

It had been good to get her thoughts off the wedding for a little while. Although Jeanie had not insisted on having the whole family at their reception, she had still not conquered all of her resentment. Her anticipated happiness had been replaced by the misery resentment always brings. Usually she could confide in Olga; but in this situation, she knew better than to complain to her. Jeanie didn't know if Olga had cherished dreams of a large wedding, but she did know they had gone off by themselves to get married. During those depression days, the simplest reception was unaffordable. Oh, they had not gone secretly or without approval and the blessing of the close relatives, but they had not been able to share their joy with them.

Jeanie smiled, remembering the winter they had stayed with her and Gram. Absorbed mostly in each other, they were unaware they were sowing dream-seeds for the little girl who observed their love. Jeanie couldn't remember Carl ever leaving to go out to the barn, to the woods, to town—anywhere—without exchanging a loving glance with Olga. Had the family been more inclined to indulge in demonstrations of affection, there certainly would have been hugs and kisses instead of that simple acknowledgment. Jeanie had been thrilled to see the way they looked at each other; just as she was when she saw Roy and Helen stroll across the yard, arm in arm. She had begun to dream of a love of her own—someday.

Jeanie began pairing and rolling the socks at the bottom of Olga's oilcloth-lined bushel basket. "Remember when the guys were working on the log house and we walked over with lunch for them. You carried a whole chocolate cream pie that mile and three-quarters in Gram's basket?"

"Oh...you would remember that!" Olga said, hiding her face behind a self-conscious, little wave as she often did. "Women in love do such impractical things!"

Jeanie longed to tell Olga how wonderful it had been to see those loving glances; how she had admired their courage through difficult times, never once hearing either of them speak negatively about the other. But, Olga was a private person, easily embarrassed, so these thoughts Jeanie kept to herself for now. Someday, perhaps, she would tell their children.

It had been a quiet afternoon with the older three children in school and little Michael napping. She would wait to see Albert, Glady and Marvin when they came home from school, but then she must hurry back. Gram would be waiting for her.

Jeanie followed her tiny aunt back to the kitchen and watched her take fragrant loaves of crusty bread from the oven and turn them out on a dishtowel.

"I know you're disappointed about the reception, but I'm glad you had the time to get over here today. See...if you were getting ready for that, you wouldn't have had time for this visit."

"I know. I hope to get to see Aunt Minnie and Aunt Gertie on Thursday. Neither one of them will be able to come to the shower tomorrow."

"Too bad. I often wonder how Minnie can care for George year after year and never complain," she shook her head, "And Gertie, who knows how sick she really is.

## Chapter Seventeen

Sometimes, when she really wants to do something, she seems strong and then...."

"I don't remember her being so concerned about her health those years you boarded with them when you taught school."

"Oh, goodness, no! She had enough energy for two people. Maybe she's alone too much; has too much time to think about her ailments. I don't know, but whatever happens, she will always be a very special person to me. I hope you will get to visit with both of them. They think a lot of you, you know."

---

The next afternoon, as each group of aunts and neighborhood ladies arrived for her shower, Jeanie grew more nervous. It was a new experience to be the center of attention.

When Ruby came, Jeanie felt more at ease and began to relax as she opened the gifts. There was a lovely chenille bedspread with pastel flowers, a shiny chrome iron from Kenny's mother, a much-needed set of dishes, several mixing bowl sets, casseroles and two bath towels. But, most treasured, were the set of wooden spoons Uncle George had carved from basswood and a wooden stool Uncle Henry had made.

When the last gift had been opened, Jeanie walked to the doorway between the two rooms where she could see them all and thanked them, tearfully, again. She wanted to say a great deal more than simply "Thank you," but emotion cut her words short.

"I suspect they did this as much for Gram's sake as for mine," Jeanie confided to Ruby over their plates of cake.

"It was for both of you," Ruby said, laugh wrinkles

crinkling at the sides of her eyes. "People enjoy helping a young couple get started."

"Yes, I guess they do. I asked Gram once if they had showers years ago. She said they didn't have them like we do now, but women shared household items and men brought seed, tools and even stock—usually at the housewarming. Remember when Uncle George and Aunt Sadie brought Carl and Olga a hen and chicks?"

"Uh-huh. That was a special gift. Eggs were precious."

"Well, I'm grateful and honored. I won't even be living here. Some of these women I may never see again."

Jeanie had no problem writing an optimistic letter to Kenny that night.

Thursday morning she packed most of the shower gifts to be shipped to their little apartment and put some of the heavier items in her room to ship later.

---

"The trees are putting on quite a show this year," Jeanie said to Roy as they drove through the brilliantly colored maple-covered hills and curves toward Ogema. "I love this stretch of road."

"Yeah, it's pretty, but there's talk about straightening it out one of these years. Too dangerous with all these curves."

When Roy dropped Jeanie off at Aunt Minnie's house, Jeanie could see her through the window hastily drying her hands. She hurried to the door, a younger version of Gram with the same type of wrap-around apron and her hair combed back in a bun, or "pug," as Gram called it.

"Oh, I'm so glad you could come today. I know it's a busy week for you. My goodness," she said, leading Jeanie into the house, "it seems like no time since you kids were

## Chapter Seventeen

*playing* wedding and here you are really getting married! Remember how my Johnny was always the groom and you were the bride and you'd get all dressed up with the old lace curtains for a veil, and I'd have to play the wedding march on the organ?"

"I sure do," Jeanie said fondly.

"Oh, let's go in here so George can visit with us," she said, leading the way to the front room with a window looking out on Ogema's main street.

George, Jeanie's cousin bedridden with a back disability for several years, grinned up at her.

"Hey!" he said, "You're lookin' good!"

Books and magazines about radio repair were stacked on the table and several radios he had been repairing sat on another table.

When Aunt Minnie invited her to have a cup of tea she declined, knowing Aunt Gertie would be waiting for her, too. She told them about the wedding plans and, when Jeanie described her dress, Aunt Minnie said she would be eager to see their pictures.

At the door, Aunt Minnie hugged her and said, "God bless you two." She took Jeanie's face between her hands and looked into her eyes. "I wish your mother could see what I'm seeing. I see a heart turned toward God."

Walking up the hill to Aunt Gertie's house, Jeanie relived that precious scene. *Oh, God! I do want to go your way!*

It had been good to see Aunt Minnie. She hadn't changed a great deal and still made no attempt to hide the large bean-sized mole on her forehead. Aunt Gertie, on the other hand, kept her hair curled and would have covered a mole in a minute.

She greeted Jeanie with a cheery, "Hi! Come in! How about a cup of coffee?"

"You bet! It smells delicious."

"I tried a new recipe," Aunt Gertie said, putting a piece of golden sponge cake on her plate. "See how you like the lemon glaze."

Aunt Gertie was always trying new recipes and usually had a few funny stories to tell. Jeanie loved to hear her deep, hearty laugh. If it weren't for the humor, it would have been unpleasant visiting with her because, more and more, she talked about her illnesses as years went by. Several years ago, she had been in a tuberculosis sanitarium for a year, but had been diagnosed early enough to make a full recovery. Now she was having trouble with her heart.

Today she had other things on her mind. Jeanie answered her questions about the shower and suddenly she said, "You sure are getting to look like your mother. She was a bit taller than you and I think her hair was darker." She shook her head. "My goodness...you're almost as old as she was when...." She did not finish the sentence.

Jeanie filled up the gap. You and Aunt Ella and Aunt Minnie are all so different. I suppose she was different from all of you."

"Yes, she was. Still, she and I were a lot alike and always had plans and a lot to talk about." She took a bite of the fluffy cake and said, "She'd sure be proud of you."

Tears sprang into Jeanie's eyes. "Do you *really* think so? I feel like I seldom do anything right."

Aunt Gertie waved that idea aside. "Oh, Gramma scolded a lot because she saw everything you did wrong, but you just forget about all that. She was so anxious to have you grow up right, she tried a little too hard. No...all I have to do is look in your eyes and I can see what direction you're headed. That's what counts, you know."

## Chapter Seventeen

Jeanie could only smile her thanks. "This cake is delicious. I like the lemon tang."

"I can't wait to see your wedding gown. I was pretty sure you'd sew it. I hope I'll feel well enough to be there," she said pensively.

"It's a mess right now after being in the suitcase. Rayon net wrinkles so badly. I'll have to iron every inch of it."

Aunt Gertie smiled, "That will be a labor of love!"

---

Riding home, enjoying the way the late afternoon sun intensified the autumn colors, Jeanie's heart soared. Both Aunt Minnie and Aunt Gertie thought her mother would be proud of her and that they could see that she was heading in the right direction, as Aunt Gertie put it.

There was a letter waiting from Kenny. He said he had moved into the apartment, which was no great task because all he had were some clothes:

> The old people are so quiet I hardly know there's anyone downstairs, but I better warn you. It isn't a quiet street. The end of the Humboldt Park el is right across the street and trains are always coming and going with their brakes screeching. The railroad is at the end of the block so there's plenty of whistle-blowing, too. And you can hear the streetcars on North Avenue, besides. To top that off, the fire station is only a couple blocks away. I'm so glad we found a nice quiet place!

That kind of noise didn't worry Jeanie. It wouldn't be like living in an apartment house with a lot of people-noise.

Friday, Aunt Ella stopped over and Jeanie tried on her gown, wrinkled as it was. She sat teary-eyed on Jeanie's bed and told her it was lovely.

Later, when Jeanie pressed the yards and yards of satin and net, she remembered that Aunt Gertie had said it would be a labor of love. Tired as she was, she was determined to make it just that.

At church that evening, Pastor Zaremba said he couldn't remember ever having a wedding rehearsal without the groom, but there was a first time for everything. Of course, the flower girl wasn't there, either.

Actually, the ceremony would be simple. Jeanie would walk down the aisle alone, right after Merle Ann. She also chose the simple form of vows where the bride and groom only had to say "yes" instead of repeating the whole thing.

There was a lot of laughter as they practiced walking down the aisle, and also back at Helen and Roy's where they had angel food cake.

Jeanie held Kenny's last letter under her pillow. Tomorrow! Tomorrow, he would come about noon and bring the flowers. That would be the last time they would ever have to say good-bye.

# 18

*Oh! No! It can't be! Not on my wedding day!* A strange, white light filled Jeanie's bedroom like after a snowstorm. Jeanie squinted at the window. The branches of the box elder tree drooped with heavy snow.

She sprang up for a better look. White everywhere. Beautiful for Christmas, but not for her wedding day! Leafy branches, unaccustomed to the added weight, bowed down to the white blanket that had been green grass just hours before.

She grabbed her old pink robe from the back of the door, pulled it on and ran downstairs.

"Oh, Mama! It couldn't snow! It just *couldn't*! Not today!"

Gram came up behind her and patted her shoulder. "Oh, it's not so bad. It's barely freezing now and the sun's coming out. You'll see! It will all be gone by four."

"But, it'll be sloppy! How are we going to get to the car? Can't you see me dragging all that satin in the snow?" she shouted in Gram's ear. "Nothing has gone right and now this!"

Tight-jawed, she glared out at the snow and then sagged down on the old iron oven door in a shivering heap. "I just don't care anymore!"

Gram grabbed her by the shoulder and gave her a rough shake. "Now you get ahold of yourself right this minute! You talk like that snow is a personal insult! So, it just happens to be your wedding day! What makes you think brides have perfect weather?"

Jeanie refused to look up.

"Well, I'm thankful plans were changed! Just think how you'd feel if we were expecting all those people for an outdoor reception this afternoon!" Gram sighed and sat down, close enough to reach Jeanie's hand. In a more gentle tone she said, "I know you've had a lot of disappointments and I wish things could have been different." She cleared her throat and squeezed Jeanie's hand. "I want you to know that I've been real proud of you through all of it. I know it hasn't been easy."

*Could she be hearing right? Gram was proud of her!*

"But now," Gram continued, "do you think it will make you feel better if you fret and fuss about the weather instead of thinking about what counts—you and Kenny?"

When Jeanie didn't answer, Gram said, "Why don't you go back to bed awhile. It's not even seven. It'll be a long day, you know."

Jeanie stood up, nodded and hugged Gram. She crept back upstairs and nestled in her bed.

Gram was right. It wouldn't do a bit of good to fret. She'd think about Kenny. In a few more hours he would be here! It seemed like they had been apart for months

## Chapter Eighteen

instead of just a week. Oh, it would be wonderful to be in his arms again. And tonight...they would be together, right here in this very bed!

And tomorrow, they'd go home...to *their home!* She wondered how Merle Ann would be on the train. Jeanie groaned. *Eight hours on a train with a three-year-old! Maybe it wasn't such a good idea to have her for our flower girl.*

She thought about having to change trains at New Lisbon with their luggage and Merle Ann. Then, at Union Station, they would have to carry it all through the station and up the escalator to the el platform; ride to the end of the Homboldt Park line; walk to their apartment, up those back stairs; drop off their luggage; then, go back and ride two streetcars to take Merle Ann home. They would probably visit a bit, ride back, climb those stairs again, and set the alarm clock for six so they would get up in time to go to work Monday. *This is not the way I thought the day after our wedding would be!*

Ah, but there were better times coming. Monday evening they would go for a hamburger after work because there was no food in the house, then go grocery shopping together. Later they would unload the big wooden box of linens, together, and maybe even rearrange some furniture. *Together!* What else mattered?

Then she remembered Gram saying she was proud of her. *That mattered!* She hugged the thought as if it were a comforting blanket.

As she drifted off to sleep, thoughts of the past summer flitted through her mind: that one fun-filled evening at the swimming pool, then walking around Logan Square with a box of popcorn, those awful days when Kenny had no job and it seemed as if he would *never* find one, and the agonizing good-byes each time they had to part. She smiled and snuggled deeper under the covers. No more good-byes.

About eleven o'clock, Jeanie saw Kenny drive in and she ran across the porch to meet him. He leaned over the big florist's box in his arm and gave her a quick kiss.

They opened the box on Gram's table.

"Ohh...!" Jeanie exclaimed as she lifted out her bouquet of roses and carnations. "Isn't it *beautiful!*" Then she saw the bridesmaid's corsages. "They're so small! I didn't know they'd be like this! Her face fell in disappointment."

"It's too late to do anything about it now," Kenny said. "Anyway this one looks pretty." He lifted out Merle Ann's little nosegay.

"Oh, it is. But, I feel so bad about the other flowers."

Carefully, they replaced them until it was time to take them to the church.

Kenny hitched himself up on Gram's table and Jeanie stood in front of him, his arms around her neck. "I missed you so much," he said and kissed her.

"Oh, you don't *know* how I missed you!" she whispered.

Between numerous kisses, Kenny told her about their trip. Merle Ann had slept a lot; Kenny, very little. Then he studied her soberly. "I hear some people think we're too young to get married."

"I wouldn't be surprised, but no one has said anything to me."

"And it sounds like you were in the middle of a mess when you got up here. Are things straightened out?"

Choosing her words carefully, Jeanie gave him a brief account of what had happened that ended by saying, "I'm not going to let it spoil our wedding! Gram reminded me that the wedding is only for a day but our marriage is for

## Chapter Eighteen

our lifetime. She said I should think about what is really important—us and our marriage."

Kenny nodded. "She's a wise lady. But I'm really sorry, because I know you wanted everyone to come back here after the ceremony."

Jeanie tried to look unconcerned. "Oh, well, they'll all be in church and quite a few will come to the wedding dance. I've got so much to tell you! Wait till you see all the shower gifts! Oh, did the big wooden box come?"

"Uh-huh, I opened it and used a couple towels. What would we do now without all the things you put away?"

Gram came in from taking water to the chickens and hugged Kenny. "You must be so tired," she said. "Are you hungry? Want a glass of milk and some coffee-*kuchen*?"

"Thanks, no. I have to get back to town," he shouted.

Jeanie walked out to the car with him. "Just think...this is the last time we have to say good-bye!"

His smile faded. "I sure hope so."

By noon, clumps of snow plopped on the soggy grass and leaves fluttered freely in the wind as if greatly relieved to be free of their burden. Jeanie felt no such relief. How would she and the girls get in and out of the car in this slush?

At Gram's insistence, Jeanie managed to eat a piece of fresh coffee-k*uchen* with jelly and drink a glass of milk.

She fussed with her hair and looked at the clock a thousand times. Was Kenny watching the clock like this?

At three, she put on her makeup and recombed her hair again. She helped Gram pin her little cameo brooch to her lace collar.

Jeanie's freshly pressed gown lay on Gram's bed.

At three-thirty she put it on.

"Oh, my!" Gram said and lifted her glasses to dab her eyes.

*She's probably wishing my mother could see me.*

She walked out of Gram's bedroom and into the next room where Ronnie hovered, waiting to be of some help.

He whistled and grinned. "Ah...kinda' thin, isn't it?"

Jeanie looked down and she could see light through her skirt. "Oh no! Look!" she shouted to Gram.

Gram disappeared into her bedroom and came out waving the full-length slip Jeanie had forgotten to put on.

Laughing with relief, Jeanie struggled out of all the yards of net and satin, put the slip on and got into the gown again. Light no longer shone through, but the skirt was a mass of wrinkles.

"What am I going to *do*? Jeanie wailed.

Gram suddenly took charge. "Ronnie, get the ironing board," she ordered. When the board was set up and the iron hot, she told Jeanie, "You walk around it and I'll press your skirt and train."

When the gown was again wrinkle free, she warned Jeanie, "Don't sit down till you get in the car."

Now it was time to put on the veil. "Oh, my bobbie pins! They're upstairs!"

Ronnie was willing to run again. "Where are they?"

"There's a new card of them on my dresser."

Soon she was pinning and pinning so the wind wouldn't blow off her veil.

When tall Bud came to the door, he leaned down and gave her a quick kiss. "Wow! Wait till your old man sees you!"

The girls and Arthur were waiting in the car that Bud had driven up close to the porch. Jeanie had only to step into it.

"I figured the heck with the grass," Bud said with a grin.

## Chapter Eighteen

At the church, cars were parked in every available place. *All these people stopped their Saturday work just for us!* Jeanie thought.

Kenny's mother was waiting in the tiny narthex with Merle Ann.

"You stay here and walk nicely," she told the little girl, "and then you can come and sit by Gramma."

Mr. Zielke, the sexton, was standing by the bell rope. "You ready for me to ring the bell?" he asked Jeanie.

The girls were in line and the guys had gone up to the altar. Jeanie nodded. "I guess so! Oh, wait a minute!" The floor was swimming with muddy slush. "Will you put down my train when I get through the doorway?"

He nodded.

She took the loops off her wrist so she would be ready to let the train down. Mr. Zielke pulled the rope and a shiver went up Jeanie's arms as the familiar old bell pealed out across the countryside.

The organist sounded the first notes of the wedding march and Ruby started down the aisle to the front of the church...to the *bare front* of the church!

*Oh no!* Jeanie inwardly groaned. She hadn't thought of flowers for the church and neither had anyone else, although and abundance of fall flowers graced neighborhood gardens. Too late now!

As she watched Pearl's precise steps, she felt her own knees begin to tremble. She tried to see Kenny, but the big old stove blocked her view. She would see him when she was walking down the aisle.

"Okay, honey, go ahead," she whispered to Merle Ann.

She didn't move. "Go ahead!" Jeanie urged a bit louder. When Jeanie stepped forward to nudge her along,

Merle Ann turned with an indignant frown and said, "You stepped on my dress!"

A titter ran through the last few pews.

Finally, Merle Ann began to walk down the aisle and Jeanie could feel her train being put down.

She had barely taken a step into the doorway when her whole body began to tremble so violently she could hardly walk. She tried to calm herself, but it was as if there were no connection between her will and her body. The fern in her bouquet picked up her every tremor.

The aisle stretched ahead as if it had somehow been lengthened. She tried to smile at Kenny, but her face felt stiff. He looked alarmed, as if he were about to run down to catch her. The tip of his nose was red, the way it always got when he was upset.

*Please God,* she prayed, *help me stop shaking.*

At last she was beside Kenny and he gripped her arm so tightly it hurt. Through a fold in her veil, Jeanie dimly saw the pastor's encouraging smile.

"Dearly beloved," he began, "we are gathered here today...."

Emma could not hear a single word, but she had felt the vibration of the organ. She had felt, too, every tremor of Jeanie's body as she came down the aisle.

*Poor little girl. All that strain had to come out somehow.*

Now, standing beside Kenny with her hand on his arm, Jeanie seemed much calmer. Though Emma could no longer see her face, it had been radiant when she had smiled at Kenny. She was sure both of them were glowing with happiness as they faced the pastor.

*My little girl is getting married!*

How could that be when it seemed like only yesterday that she had brought her home as a baby?

*Oh, if only Emmie could see her now!* She was sure

*Chapter Eighteen*

Emmie would feel as she did. This marriage was ordained by God.

*Heavenly Father, bless these, thy children,* Emma prayed. *Please keep them together for many, many years. Make their love grow stronger with each passing year.*

"With this ring, I thee wed," Kenny said, slipping the ring on her finger.

They had just spoken their vows, and now Jeanie felt as if those vows were solemnly sealed.

"I now pronounce you man and wife," said the pastor.

Jeanie felt a sudden surge of joy.

"You may kiss your bride," the pastor quietly told Kenny.

Tenderly, they kissed their first married kiss. Then, they exchanged triumphant smiles.

When they turned, there was Gram's happy—and proud—smile beaming up at them. As the first notes of the recessional rang through the little church, Jeanie didn't care if others thought they were too young to get married. Gram, she knew, believed their love would endure.

To order additional copies of

## Satin in the Snow

please send $9.95*
plus $3.95 shipping and handling to:

Barnes Enterprises
3061 Bible Union Rd.
Martin, TN 38237

or to order by phone,
have your credit card ready and call

**1-800-917-BOOK**

*Quantity Discounts are Available